NO TIME
TO DIE

by

BUCK STIENKE

THE AUTHOR

 Buck is a native Texan from Houston. He moved to the Texas Hill Country when he was ten and found rural living to his liking. Following his graduation from the USAF Academy, he flew single and multi-engine jets, and multi-engine recip aircraft for the Air Force before a twenty-five year commercial airline career. In addition to flying, his interests have included ranching, playing professional football, long range shooting, gourmet cooking, singer-songwriter, sporting good retail, big game hunting, gunsmithing, machinist, and suppressor design and manufacturing. His writings often reflect these interests.

ISBN-13: 978-1-7329119-8-7
ISBN-10: 1-7329119-8-3

Timber Creek Press
Imprint of Timber Creek Productions, LLC
312 N. Commerce St.
Gainesville, Texas 76240

Published by: Timber Creek Press
timbercreekpresss@yahoo.com
www.timbercreekpress.net
Twitter: @pagact
Facebook Book Page:
www.facebook.com/TimberCreekPress

DEDICATION

This book is dedicated to the brave men who fought on both sides of the conflict now known as the American Civil War. It is not possible for us to accurately judge them using today's standards of morality and justice—one hundred and fifty years of hindsight is never twenty-twenty, falling victim to the revisionist actions of "historians" with an agenda, so called "social justice warriors", and a mainstream media who may actually hate America.

Tearing down historical monuments dedicated to the memory of common soldiers fighting for their individual states and brothers in arms is sacrilege.

ACKNOWLEDGMENT

I want to sincerely thank Lt. Col. Clyde DeLoach, USMC (ret), retired English Professor Terry D. Heflin, and my good friend and fellow author Ken Farmer for their fabulous work in editing this book.

TIMBER CREEK PRESS

CHAPTER ONE

NORTHEAST ARKANSAS

July 15, 1863

"Light the fuses, boys … that Yankee train will be here in thirty seconds," the lanky Confederate lieutenant colonel ordered.

He backed the spirited lineback dun stallion away from the elevated roadbed and into the towering loblolly pines that lined both sides of the remote section of track.

"You got it, Colonel," replied the master sergeant who had supervised the laying of the black powder charges.

Four enlisted men scratched the wooden lucifers they carried against the shiny polished top surface of the steel rails—phosphorous and sulfur responded to the friction and burst into flame as the nervous soldiers touched them to the intentionally frayed ends of the identical fuses.

Each lit off with a continuous hiss that sounded like an angry rattlesnake preparing to strike, complete with a small tendril of smoke that curled up in the humid still air.

They sprinted to their horses being held by other members of the Second Battalion of Texas Cavalry, grabbed the reins and mounted up without delay.

Each knew the total of thirty-two pounds of explosives buried under the rails would be more than enough to do what the planner of the military expedition had in mind. None of them wanted to become a casualty from flying debris.

They wheeled about and rode into the woods on the inside of the gradual turn and waited.

As the summer sun set, the engineer in the Union Army troop train checked his pocket watch. The fancy gold timepiece—complete with an embossed image of the 6-4-2 wood-fired steam engine that pulled the twelve cars—indicated it was almost 7 PM.

Looks like another on-time arrival in Little Rock. He wound the stem six times and dropped the fancy gift from the railroad president back into his bib overalls.

Elliott R. Patterson was a dedicated company man. Fourteen years on the job, and he had never had an accident.

His on-time record was second to none in the company, and this milk run from Saint Louis to Little Rock was like so many others he had made. Coming down the steep grade in the Ozarks, he had pulled off a little on the power, letting gravity do the work.

Patterson knew the tracks leveled off as they came out of the turn to the west and nudged the Johnson bar forward a bit.

He checked the gauge on the boiler and saw what his ears had already told him. The increased power demand he asked for was being transferred to the pistons working furiously beneath the deck of the glistening black cab.

The essentially coasting train began to pick up even more speed under its own power as he called out to his fireman, "Willis, feed this big boy if we are ever gonna make it to the station on time."

"Break time's over, I reckon." The thirty-five year old native of Indiana wiped his damp brow with a red and blue paisley print bandana and stuffed it in his back pocket of his faded overalls.

The midsummer temperature didn't need any help at all from the engine's firebox to make a man break into a sweat. He used a hooked poker to lift the latch on the thick cast iron door and chunked a few pieces of seasoned oak into the hellish compartment.

Temperatures in the engine cab rose to 140 degrees for a few seconds before he slammed the door closed and flipped the latch back into place. "There you go, ER ... Does that make you a happy man?"

Patterson nodded and lit a carved cherry wood pipe and drew in a deep breath of the pungent smelling tobacco as the rails ahead curved gracefully westward. He exhaled a plume of blue-gray smoke into the fifty miles per hour breeze whistling past the cab and squinted as the golden rays of the setting sun reflected off the twin ribbons of steel.

He blinked his eyes twice and pulled his head back inside, trying to readjust his vision from the temporary sun blindness.

One fuse set off its eight pound charge a full second before the others. A joint where two sections of track were attached was blasted upward, twisted and separated by over a foot.

Captain Doran Ingrham cursed the early detonation—a full eighty yards in front of the train's cowcatcher. He needn't have worried, as the relatively heavy train would have taken a quarter mile to slow to a stop under the best of circumstances.

As he watched, the other blasts thundered their way through the roadbed and sent splinters and chunks of burning creosote-soaked railroad ties up into the undercarriage of the engine's wood tender, three passenger cars, and the third freight car.

Without the outer rail in place to hold the train to the curve, the centrifugal force of the train cars forced them to drop off the inner rail as well. One by one, they began to tilt as they derailed, sending showers of crushed limestone rocks flying off the rapidly spinning cast iron wheels.

The coupling between the engine and tender released and the fully laden car tipped over, dumping its top-heavy load of firewood as it barreled into the trees with a mighty crash that reverberated through the virgin forest.

ER Patterson yanked back on the Johnson bar and hit the brakes, instantly locking the drive wheels on Engine number 29 with a high-pitched screech that could be heard for miles.

One second later, the shiny pride of the Union Pacific railroad crossed over the torn apart rail joint and vaulted off the five foot high roadbed into the waist deep brush that had grown alongside the track.

He and his fireman screamed as the engine plowed though the underbrush and careened into the woods—landing upright and continued barreling into the forest as the cast iron cowcatcher caromed off of some four foot thick trees and snapped off other smaller ones with impunity.

Union soldiers riding in the passengers cars had been playing cards, chatting up one another with war stories of real and imagined heroism from their battles in the never-ending war.

However, as the flimsy cars accordioned into each other, crushed and twisted in all directions in the blink of an eye, the only sounds that could be heard above the tortured tune of agonized metal shearing and wood splintering were the cries of men and boys screaming out in stark terror and pain.

Damnation ... worked better than I thought it would. Lt. Colonel Eric Schmidt mused as he watched the mayhem that his surprise attack on the enemy troop train had created.

He pulled the double barreled muzzle loading shotgun from it custom-made leather scabbard—an accouterment years ahead of its time—hand crafted by his late father.

"Bugler, sound the attack!"

The young corporal from Tyler blew the notes for the nearly three hundred men to initiate their charge.

The signal was repeated by two other company buglers and followed almost immediately with a chorus of rebel yells designed to instill fear in the enemy.

The impassioned high-pitched bloodcurdling yelps—reminiscent of several bands of coyotes howling—worked.

Most of the survivors of the train wreck opted to give up to the hordes of gray clad cavalrymen that descended upon them like vengeful locusts.

Others who dared to bring weapons to bear on the volunteers from Texas fell in a furious fuselage of pistol and rifle fire at close range.

Eric tapped his heels to Bucky's ribs, urging the dun to break from the safety of the dark timber and lope up and across the roadbed.

He reined him right to clear the cloud of steam venting from the boiler seam where a missing row of rivets told of an unanticipated steel plate flexing caused by the derailment. *Good thing. The last thing we need is a steam explosion while we check this wreck for supplies.*

NO TIME TO DIE

The Union naval blockade of the Mississippi and the ports all along the Gulf coast had left the Confederacy woefully short of necessities. Intercepting enemy supply wagons, trains and barges was one way to try to tip the scales.

Movement at the back of the engine caught his attention. A man wearing faded blue overalls staggered to the platform and held on to his midsection.

Willis caught sight of the Confederate officer holding a shotgun leveled at him and raised his hands up—away from the second degree burns that he suffered when he had been thrown forward against the closed firebox door during the crash. The soldier motioned for him to step down and he readily complied.

Schmidt waved him to continue back toward the rest of the cars and didn't catch the sight of the second man peeking around the door frame at the back of the cab until it was too late.

The engineer's hat was missing and a fresh gash above his eyes spoke of his harsh contact with some hard object. Blood ran down his nose and dripped across the front of his overalls, but that didn't stop him from pulling a Colt .36 caliber pistol from his left rear pocket and taking a shot at the mounted rebel commander.

Eric wheeled the scattergun around and fired as the railroad man pulled the trigger. The two shots rang out as one, with acrid sulfurous gunsmoke belching out in both directions.

The load of 00 buckshot lifted Patterson off his feet and sprayed his brains across the rear of his beloved Engine number 29. His body slid backwards off the platform and disappeared on the far side.

"Colonel! You all right?" shouted one of his senior NCOs.

"Yeah … Lucky for me he could not shoot worth a…"

His reply was cut short as his mount took a couple of steps backwards and then lurched to the side. *Oh my God … Bucky.*

He released the reins and swung his right leg over the high cantle of his McClellen saddle and hopped out of the left stirrup on to the rock strewn side of the tracks.

Keeping one hand on his horse, he eased around the front to see a small hole in the buckskin's chest. Frothy bright red bubbles dripped from its nose and a thin streak of crimson ran down between his legs. Bucky's eyes were wide with fear as he tried to process what ailment had befallen him.

"Easy boy, take it easy," he said as he stroked the stallion's neck. "Gotta calm down, Bucky. Everything is gonna be…"

The magnificent horse's knees buckled as it eyes rolled back.

Eric tried to hold him up, but there was nothing anyone could have done. Shot though the aorta, his much loved horse had died as a cavalryman's mount in combat.

The twenty one year old soldier was devastated. He had treasured the animal for ten years, ever since its birth and never owned another. Tears rimmed his eyes as his first sergeant dismounted and stepped closer.

"Colonel … sir, we got things to do, sir … I will have one of the men strip your gear, and have a replacement mount brought up."

Eric wiped back the tears with the back of his gloved hand as he got to his feet. "Do that, Sergeant

Major. Take that man into custody," he said, pointing at the injured fireman. "See to his wounds."

He laid the shotgun down beside his fallen horse and drew a Remington .44 caliber sixgun from his hip. Turning back toward the wrecked engine, he strode off purposefully.

Sporadic gunfire had almost dissipated when he reached the back of the still steaming engine and cautiously looked around the far side.

The engineer's body was lying upside down on the steps up to the platform. Beside him lay the Colt revolver.

Eric picked up the six shooter and slipped it under his uniform belt. He took one last look at the what remained of the face of the man that had tried to kill him.

Schmidt burned the image into his memory. *Sorry dumb bastard ... You just could not leave well enough alone, could you?*

He started to turn away, but the glint of a flash of gold from the front of the man's overalls caught his attention.

Eric reached down and withdrew a gold timepiece, complete with a solid gold chain. He examined the embossed cover and then turned it over to read the short inscription engraved on the back.

To ER Patterson
For long and faithful service.

He tucked the watch into his tunic and looked at the sightless brown eyes staring back up at him. *Nowhere near enough an even trade for my Bucky, but I reckon it is all you had.*

Eric looked back to the wreckage of the train where his men had Union soldiers crawling out of the demolished cars with their hands up. Several were being relieved of their sidearms. He took in a deep breath and let it out slowly.

CHAPTER TWO

NORTHEAST ARKANSAS

The senior surviving Union Army officer—an infantry major from Illinois who had been seated in the third passenger car—was somewhat taken back by the youthful appearance of the Confederate Lieutenant Colonel. *That whippersnapper cannot be much out of his teens.*

The shaken and bruised soldier came to attention and looked up at the much larger blond haired rebel, who stood at least six feet three, and was even taller in his riding boots. His gray woolen uniform didn't do a thing to hide his broad shoulders.

A shock of blonde hair hung down past his collar, and a full mustache added a modicum of maturity to his youthful countenance.

A Union issued Ames cavalry saber dangled off his left side, behind a second .44 caliber revolver that matched the well used one in his right hand.

"Major Oliver C. Winthorpe, Fourteenth Infantry Battalion. May I have the pleasure knowing who has the honor to accept my offer of surrender?"

Eric holstered his Remington, butt forward, and lowered the black leather flap. He removed his right riding gauntlet, tucked it into his belt and extended his bare hand.

"Most certainly, Major. I am Lieutenant Colonel Eric Schmidt, Commander of the Second Regiment, Texas Cavalry."

The major stared at the much younger man for an instant, but the Texan's blue eyes did not yield a glimmer of warmth.

He took the proffered hand and shook it firmly, the physical strength of the victorious leader unmistakable.

"My men will afford your troops the protection of the rules of war as pertain to your current status as prisoners. Do you, by chance, have a doctor with you?"

Winthorpe shook his head. "We have only replacement infantry for the post in Little Rock."

A brief frown crossed Eric's face. "That is indeed unfortunate. We shall, of course, endeavor to offer treatment for your injured, within our somewhat austere medical capability."

"My men and I would be deeply gratified by your generosity, sir."

Colonel Schmidt nodded. "It is the Christian thing to do, Major. I do not hate you, personally … but you are indeed my sworn enemy. If your troops cooperate fully with my men as prisoners of war, then you all shall have an excellent chance to live out this bloody conflict Mister Lincoln has thrust upon us."

His blue eyes narrowed. "I must however advise you, sir, that any attempt to escape will result in summary execution."

Major Winthorpe swallowed hard—the dryness in his throat made it far more difficult than usual.

There was no uncertainty in the victorious Confederate officer's voice.

The major came to attention and snapped a crisp salute. Eric returned it smartly, and then spun around.

Captain Ingrham watched and listened to the exchange from a few feet away as his cavalrymen kept their rifles leveled at the survivors.

Our colonel learned all that there diplomacy falderdal from that West Pointer, all right. Told me how those officers are taught to treat each other with respect ... right after just a trying to kill each other as best they could. Cannot for the life of me figure out why.

"Doran, take charge of the good major here and see that he and the prisoners are properly disarmed. Have Whitman and Stevens do what they can for the wounded. You know my standing orders about escape."

"Yes, sir. Shall handle it." He smiled broadly, his long gray hair tied back in a ponytail that hung far below his slouch hat.

Ingrham had a slim but muscular physique and bright blue eyes that sparkled when he talked. He was a few years older than his commander and possessed a vast knowledge of training horses. His tactical field experience fighting plains Indians for the Texas Rangers was an asset his commander used frequently.

"Send someone down to the crossing to bring up the wagons, if you please."

Ingrham cracked a wide west Texas grin. "Already a step ahead of you, Colonel. 'Bout three minutes ago, I reckon."

A slight smile came to Schmidt's face. "Knew I could count on you … Carry on."

Eric made his way past the lines of captured Union soldiers, acknowledging his own men with a slight nod as he continued to the next to the last car in the wrecked train. It was still upright, but the last car had uncoupled and rolled once it left the track. Shattered pieces of painted lumber lay beneath the steel axles.

Intelligence gathered from a southern spy working in Memphis had been relayed via telegraph through Little Rock. He wanted to see exactly how accurate the information had been. Three of his cavalrymen held four railroad workers at gunpoint.

One civilian was dressed in bloody overalls—the result of a scalp wound—the other three in dark charcoal suits.

Eric addressed the injured man. "Must have been in the caboose. Anybody else with you?"

"Well, sir, they was two of us, but Albert musta broke his neck when the car derailed. Never had no chance a'tall." Tears filled his eyes.

The colonel glanced at a young redheaded corporal. "Get this man up there with the walking wounded. Come back here when you are done."

"Yessir. Mister … you heard the man. Move on out and step lively," he said with an east Texas drawl.

One look down the muzzle of the .58 caliber Enfield rifle was more than enough to encourage the injured brakeman to comply without question.

Eric eyed the three men who had been sent to guard the shipment of cash to Little Rock. "Well, now … which one of you intrepid souls knows the combination to the safe?"

They looked nervously at each other. The youngest one was Ezekiel Matthews, a twenty four year old native of Saint Louis, with a clean shaven face and freckles from a youth spent in the summer sun. He was obviously scared from the aftermath of the crash and now the prospect of somehow becoming a Confederate prisoner of war. His lower lip twitched nervously. He searched for reassurance in the eyes of the older former Saint Louis police officers, now serving as railroad security personnel.

One with dark brown muttonchop sideburns tinged with gray shook his head almost imperceptibly. The other one was holding an injured left arm and scowled. His balding head sported a couple of red scrapes, and his bushy black mustache perfectly framed his down turned lips in an inverted U shape. His eyes narrowed slightly as he glared at the newly hired guard.

Eric watched their reactions without missing a single subtle clue. "Gents, we don't have all day, and I do need to check the contents of the safe inside that car. We can do this one of two ways. The easy way…"

"I want to speak to my engineer," the man with the huge sideburns interrupted.

"What is your name?" Schmidt shot back.

"Jones … Thadius Jones. I demand to speak to my engineer."

Eric grinned, but it was a sardonic smile if one could call it that. He slipped his hand inside his uniform tunic.

"Mister Jones, you can demand all you want ... But unless you can speak to the great beyond ... your ER Patterson will not be hearing you... Not in this lifetime."

He slipped the golden pocket watch out and thumbed the cover open. "My, my ... how time flies. You Yankees have three minutes."

He snapped the timepiece cover closed and then shot a side glance at Ezekiel.

The youngest guard gasped audibly, and his knees began to wobble.

The older two stared at the watch for a second and recognized it immediately.

Jones locked eyes with his younger captor. His back stiffened a bit. "Three minutes until what?"

"Three minutes until we start the hard way." The rebel commanding officer's voice had suddenly taken a colder, far more menacing tone.

The master sergeant observing the interaction had been with the Second Battalion since early late 1861 and had witnessed the rise of the brilliant young officer since he first came into contact with the Confederate forces as a teenager—out to seek retribution for his parent's death at the hands of a Yankee patrol.

Woody Williams had been in Shreveport when Lieutenant Schmidt interrogated a Union prisoner of war and bluffed his way to getting the critical information needed to locate and capture the remnants of a larger enemy force.

"Colonel! Colonel! Can I skin 'em this time? That there custom made pig sticker you took offen that Yankee soldier what killed yore sister done a real fine job!"

Eric shot a quick glance over at the sergeant. "If you promise to clean it thoroughly afterwards. You know how I would surely and purely hate to see that blade rust."

He reached back for the black leather scabbard partially hidden behind the holster on his right hip and slipped the knife free.

In a touch of theatrics, he twisted the Bowie knife blade slowly as if he were inspecting the razor sharp edge, all the while holding onto the deeply furrowed stag handle.

The rays of the setting sun glinted off the blade—the reflection shone like the fires of hell on Eric's face. His sky blue eyes narrowed into mere slits as his handsome face turned into a demon possessed.

At least that is what young Ezekiel Matthews saw. His bladder let go as his eyes rolled back in his head. The young man's knees buckled, and he toppled to the railroad right of way, landing in a fetal position on the rocks.

"Leave him lay," Eric ordered as he caught Woody's eyes. "Here you go, Master Sergeant … Catch."

He flipped the knife in slow turns, end-over-end. Woody released his left hand from the fore stock of his rifle and snatched the stag handle like a timber rattlesnake striking.

Eric rested his right hand on his revolver butt. "Two minutes."

The balding guard began to breath faster and faster, almost like a dog panting. "Tell 'im, Thadius! These crazy rebels will skin us for shore!"

"Shut your trap! They would not dare," he snapped back.

Woody broke into a laugh. "Funny thing, mister, but them's the same words that Yankee corporal said ... just before that man standing right there skint him alive ... Pitiful sight, I tell you what. You coulda heard him a screaming all the way to Monroe." He shook his shoulders for effect.

"Thadius! Damn you to hell! It ain't yore money in thar! Go on and tell 'im!" His voice had risen almost a whole octave. Tears streamed down his face.

Thadius Jones licked his parched lips, and then stared at the knife in the hand of the rebel sergeant. He watched as Woody tossed his rifle to the returning corporal and transferred the edged instrument to his right hand.

Eric made a dramatic point by opening the railroad timepiece with a bit of a dramatic flourish.

He glanced at the watch face, and then at the guard. "Sixty seconds, Mister Jones, and then your body and soul belong to Master Sergeant Williams ... Choose wisely."

The hired man felt his heart pounding away, almost as if it were somehow trying to escape without him. His own breathing became much more rapid and shallow.

He stared at the knife, then back to the sergeant's face, and back to the knife. *Damnation! It is not my money, and they do not leave me no choice. They did not pay me to let some savage animals skin me alive!*

Ten more seconds passed. Woody waved the knife back and forth as if to hypnotize the condemned man.

He broke into a huge evil grin, exposing tobacco stained teeth. He turned slightly to one side and let fly a stream of Beech Nut juice. "What is it gonna be … railroad man?"

Jones had never felt so alone or so vulnerable in his life. All thought of bravery and duty had fled his mind, leaving him suddenly colder and weaker than he could ever remember.

He felt his life's blood pounding at his temples. He licked his lips once more.

Lt. Colonel Schmidt made a show of looking at the watch one more time. He shot a side glance at Woody and then locked eyes with Jones. "Time is up."

The color in his flushed face seemed to fade instantly. "I'll open the consarned box! Just keep that maniac away from me!"

"Wise choice, Mister Jones," Eric said as he held out his hand.

Williams stepped closer and handed him his knife.

He took it and slipped it back in its leather sheath without even looking. Eric pointing at the passed out railroad guard. "Get that one on his feet and escort the pair of them up front with the others prisoners."

"Yessir." Two of the soldiers grabbed the prone man under the arms and stood him up. "Wake up, boy. You ain't dead." He slapped the unconscious guard on the cheek, arousing him from his fainting spell.

They led them away as Eric and Woody followed Jones into the cargo car. It was tilted at an precarious angle on the slope of the railway bed. The sliding outer door was still left ajar as it was when he and his coworkers had jumped out.

§§§

CHAPTER THREE

ARKANSAS RAIL LINE

Once inside, it was obvious that the cargo had shifted quite a bit during the derailment. Barrels of molasses were knocked over and piled up against crates of canned goods, known as seal tights.

Two large sacks of flour had slid off a stack and partially covered the green painted three foot by three foot express safe. Eric grabbed one sack by the corner and lifted it as it were a pillow, setting it back on the pile.

"Open her up."

Jones did as ordered. The door to the express safe swung wide after he entered the combination and swung the handle ninety degrees.

Inside, a dozen stacks of fresh union currency and two cloth bags occupied the bottom half. A thin metal shelf held a handful of manila envelopes stuffed with bills of lading for the other cargo which filled the remainder of the two cargo cars.

Thadius sank back onto the floor and exhaled deeply.

"Sergeant Williams, take Mister Jones up to join his fellows, and have my new horse and six wagons brought around. Want this all loaded up before dark, if at all possible."

"You betcha, Colonel. Come on, Jones ... Today is yore lucky day."

He shot a look at the rough country soldier. *You think so? I got train wrecked, captured by Johnny Rebs and damn near skinned alive. You call that lucky, do you now?* He never said a word, careful not to press his luck, as if he had any left at all.

Eric lifted one of the two bags of coins. *Rather heavy. Must weigh close to forty pounds. Wonder if it is silver or gold?* It was marked Philadelphia Mint.

He drew his knife and carefully slit part of the thread stitching up one end on the foot long bag. Slipping the knife back into its sheath, he wiggled his index and middle fingers between the folded layers of the off-white canvas cloth.

He spread his fingers apart and got a glimpse inside. *Oh my God. Gold, not silver.* Eric grabbed one coin by the edge and pulled it out. The profile of a lady wearing a crown—called a coronet—filled one side. The Great Seal of the United States was embossed on the back, along with the words *TWENTY D.*

There is a small fortune in just these two sacks. He slipped the twenty dollar gold piece back in with its brethren. *Need something to disguise this, at least until I get back to base camp. Far too much of a temptation for most folks I know.*

His eyes raced around the jumbled box car and found a perfect camouflage—a torn sack of beans. He dumped out part of the dried pintos and stuffed the sack of coins inside, tying the top off in a single overhand knot.

His belt knife quickly converted a second sack into a suitable hiding place, and he chunked both out into the brush alongside the tracks.

Eric stepped down out of the cargo car and looked back to the west. The first of the freight wagons the battalion owned was coming into view around the bend. *Good timing lads. Let us get this business done with and make our way back south.*

Master Sergeant Williams rode up, with the lead rope of a high spirited jet black stallion in his hands. Larger than most of the unit's mounts, the sleek, well muscled steed stood over sixteen hands tall.

Eric recognized his saddle, tack, and shotgun butt sticking out of the scabbard. For a second, the sight of Bucky lying in the railway clearing floated past, but he willed the painful image away as he reached for the reins.

"What is his name?"

Woody handed over the leather ribbons. "Captain Ingrham trained him himself, sir. Called him Black Thunder, but I reckon you can call him whatever pleases you, Colonel."

"Black Thunder it is." Eric then ground tied the horse—basically dropping the reins exactly where he wanted the horse to stay.

He patted the new mount on its neck and whispered to its left ear. "My name is Eric. We are gonna make it though this thing together, you and me."

He rubbed the horse's muzzle and let him smell his scent. "This is me, Thunder."

Thunder licked him and then nodded his head as if to say hello. That brought a fresh smile to the rebel commander.

"Woody, pass the word. Any Yankee who volunteers to help load out the wagons gets to ride. Those prisoners that do not, have to walk out of here."

"Consider it done, sir." He wheeled around and loped back up the tracks.

Eric unstrapped the covers on his saddle bags, walked over and retrieved both of the heavy sacks containing the unissued gold pieces from their temporary hiding places.

"Here you go, big boy. You get to make yourself useful, and we have not even left yet."

Forty minutes later, the salvaged dry goods and captured Union weapons were loaded aboard the first six freight wagons each pulled by a team of four horses.

Another eight wagons and three buckboards were lined up to accept the prisoners of war.

Eric met with the union commander and pulled him aside. "Major Winthorpe, I would ask that you choose six men to stay behind as a burial detail for your dead and to provide medical aid for your severely wounded and injured. They would not likely survive the rigors of a trip with us. We shall leave adequate food and water for their needs until the expected recovery expedition arrives from Little Rock."

The look on the Union officer's face was a somber one. He glanced over his shoulder at the remnants of his battalion. "It is at times like this that the rigors of command weigh heavy on a man's soul. Told to hold another one's future in your hands, not knowing which choice is best, can make a man old before his time."

Schmidt merely nodded in agreement.

"But you knew that already, I suppose. My apologies, Colonel. I will make those assignments."

He extended his hand. Eric shook it firmly as their eyes met.

"Thank you again, sir, for your humanitarian gesture. My men and I appreciate it."

"You are most welcome, sir. Would like to think that your army would reciprocate in kind, were our positions reversed."

Winthorpe nodded but said nothing more. He released his grip and exhaled heavily. He turned and walked to rejoin his men.

Ten minute's later, the first freight wagon loaded with captured Yankee troops—along with it cavalry escort—rolled out along the railroad right of way.

When the last one followed, surrounded by another squad of Confederate cavalry, the Union sergeant left behind to lead the burial detail spat out a brown stream of tobacco juice, and then wiped his chin on the back of his gloved hand.

He leaned on one of the half dozen shovels left behind by the victorious force. "Count yer blessin's boys. Them rebel prison camps ain't no bed of roses, I tell you what … We best get these here bodies under ground, afore they take to stinkin'."

The summer sun was an orange ball setting fire to the Arkansas horizon as the sizable convoy of wagons and Confederate cavalry exited the tree line terminating at the flood plain of the Mississippi River.

Scouts ranged far ahead of the column, keeping an eye out for any Union patrol that might, by some manner of ill timing, happen to cross paths with the retreating southerners.

Major Winthorpe had been given one of the reserve horses and was spared the bone jarring ride in a freight wagon. He accompanied Eric Schmidt and the brigade first sergeant.

The major turned in the saddle and looked back at the string of wagons and then turned back around.

Eric studied the man's face for a moment. "Something wrong, Major?"

The Union officer had been mostly silent for the early part of the trip.

He glanced over at Eric. "Sorry, Colonel. I was merely contemplating the fate of my command ... Wondering if you planned to press on all night in the dark. How you planned to feed such a gaggle … that sort of thing."

Eric grinned. "Expect I would do the same in your position. In about a mile, we shall come upon a shallow swale, or depression if you will. It is dry this time of year and I pre positioned my cooks and our overnight camp in there. They should have a hot meal ready upon our arrival."

"That explains why I couldn't see a camp up ahead. My compliments on your strategic planning."

"May not have been at this war business for long, but I do catch on quickly."

Winthorpe nodded. "That you do, sir. May I be so impertinent as to inquire if you are a West Point man? You seem to be well educated for a young officer."

Eric shook his head. "Take that as a compliment, sir. One of my immediate superiors and mentors was a graduate, but as for myself … I was home schooled in a log house in the piney woods of east Texas. My mother was a voracious reader and apparently quiet adept at teaching."

"How interesting. That is impressive, indeed. Please feel free to pass on my regards."

The grin faded from the younger officer's face. "That, unfortunately, will not be possible. My mother, along with my father and sister were murdered by a Yankee cavalry patrol a little over a year ago."

"My deepest apologies, sir. Never meant to open any personal wounds."

Lieutenant Colonel Schmidt shook his head. "No offense taken, Major. Day by day, I am learning to deal with the emotional aspects of my personal loss. War is a nasty business, replete with many new opportunities to mourn. Do not know that I would have chosen to enter the profession of arms under other circumstances."

The Union officer studied Eric's face as he turned to scan at the eastern horizon. "Did your family own many slaves?"

Eric head snapped around. "Slaves? No Schmidt has ever owned a slave." He turned and pointed back at the column. "In my regiment, only three of my men come from families that own slaves. It is just not that commonplace as some would think. I do know some cotton plantation owners that utilize slave labor, but they are, in fact, expensive to buy, feed, house, and keep secure … notwithstanding the moral issue. You may not be aware, but back in Texas, we voted against secession twice before it passed." He let that point sink in.

"My commander and mentor is a graduate of West Point. He tells me that only four percent of the slaves that ever left Africa came here to North America. The vast majority of them went to former Spanish colonies in Central America, sugar plantations in the Caribbean or to Brazil. "

Winthorpe sat mute for a short time as he processed the colonel's unexpected reply. "Perhaps there is more to this conflict than the northern papers imply."

"We have a few days ride ahead of us to discuss the political ramifications of the War of Northern Aggression, as we know it. Have had the opportunity to ask questions of far more experienced businessmen and politically astute senior officers. In our rustic rural ranch house, we paid little attention to the Washington politics and tariffs on raw cotton exports." A slight grin crossed his face.

"Apparently, tax revenues levied upon those cotton products of slave labor … the very same practice so abhorred by you northerners … were the greatest source of income to your federal government. Some of my mentors claim that the real reason Mister Lincoln embarked upon this calamity was that your government would be essentially bankrupt without the egregious tariffs placed upon our southern exports."

Thoughts inside the major's head were spinning. "I shall look forward to our continued conversations."

Eric nodded and scanned the horizon ahead once more.

§§§

CHAPTER FOUR

SHERMAN, TEXAS

The tall, muscular black man moved through the densely wooded bottom land without making a sound. His dark eyes slowly scanned the vegetation as he stepped over a fallen red oak tree and gently touched down the ball of his bare right foot on the other side.

He licked his lips and thought about the canteen tied to his saddle on the huge brown and black mule he had hobbled almost a half mile away.

The flicker of motion at the edge of the clearing caught his attention. He froze for a moment, his trailing leg only inches above the rotting log. Unconsciously, the twenty-four year old Bass Reeves even stopped breathing for a moment. His eyes focused forty yards ahead as he balanced with the double barreled shotgun held close to his chest. The head of a white tail doe appeared as the deer stepped forward and began to graze on the forbs growing at the edge of the field of cotton.

Her head was turned away from his direction. She took another step, exposing more of her head and neck past a large sycamore tree that grew at the edge of the fertile creek bottom.

That must be the one they done tol' me 'bout. Ain't got no little ones with her. Bass eased his left foot to the ground as his pulse rate began to quicken. Ever so slowly, he lifted the muzzle of the shotgun as he eased the buttstock to his shoulder.

The wind that had been nearly calm since the sun broke the horizon picked up slightly from the south. Bass could hear the distant singing of a Negro spiritual from a handful of fellow slaves as they laboriously chopped weeds in the seemingly endless rows of cotton.

He mouthed the words to their plaintive song as he brought the brass bead sight to his aim point, just below the barren doe's head. "Swing low, sweet chariot, coming for to carry me …"

The early morning tranquility was shattered by the blast of the 12 gauge muzzle loader. The smoke from the round momentarily obscured his vision of the deer. Her death was instantaneous.

As the smoke drifted back into the deeper woods, Bass could see the deer lying near the field's edge.

He stepped quickly to his prey, with his right hand on the bowie knife in a sheath in the rear pocket of his overalls. It was not needed to finish off the kill.

The heavy buckshot load had done its work well, breaking the neck and spine cleanly without wasting any meat. He laid the shotgun down in the short grass. It had done its job, but Bass' master, George Robertson Reeves, only loaded the shotgun or rifle shortly before each hunt and never gave him powder, shot, and ball for a second round.

Bass patted the doe on the shoulder. She was in excellent shape, but for some unknown reason had not produced a fawn crop that year.

His deep, rich, voice reflected his southern dialect, having moved from Tennessee to Texas when he was but eight years old.

"Well, girl, you did not die in vain. Me and them other folk gonna treat you real nice, we are."

He looked to the heavens. "Lord Jesus, thank you for this day and for bringing us this here fine animal of yours for us to eat. 'Preciate your bounty and goodness ... in Jesus' name we pray, amen."

After he reached the mule, Bass tied the deer carcass to brass rings on the saddle skirt.

When he was done, he lifted the canteen off the saddle horn and took a long drink. He washed the last traces of blood smears off of the knife blade and slipped it back into the leather sheath.

Carefully, he rinsed the partially dried reddish-brown blood off of his large and powerful hands before his wiped them on his overalls.

Reeves retrieved his well-worn slouch boots from the saddle bags, dusted the black clay soil off of his feet and put them on.

Finally, he removed the hobbles from the mule's front legs and tossed them into the left saddle bag.

Grabbing the reins, he stabbed his boot into the steel stirrup and swung up into the saddle. "Come on, Cletus. Git up there. You gots to earn your feed, too ... same as me."

He smiled at his own little joke as the sixteen hand mule broke into a trot.

His bushy black mustache partially hid his white even teeth. *Massa George gonna be happy with me today. Got that big ol' doe with just one shot, jest like he showed me.*

SHREVEPORT, LOUISIANA

The midmorning sun framed the gorgeous twenty year old red haired girl perfectly as she entered the post office a half block off the Texas Street main thoroughfare. Other patrons glanced her way—the menfolk were drawn to her wasp waist, sea green eyes, finely chiseled features and perfect alabaster skin.

Two ladies studied her bespoke floor length dress and one whispered to her equally jealous friend, "I wonder how much that set her father back?"

The taller one, a thirty two year old brunette, shook her head. "I would not pretend to make a supposition on that matter, but I can state without hesitation that Mister Augustin LeBlanc can easily afford it. My father says that he is the wealthiest man in this part of Louisiana."

The younger woman approached the rows of individual mail boxes and opened her embroidered handbag. She unsnapped a small metal clasp on a side pocket, retrieved a small cast iron skeleton key, and opened the lock securing the oaken door. "Oh my, so many this time," she said softly as she began to empty the flat cardboard boxes into a cloth shopping bag.

"Need a hand there, Miss Angelina?"

She turned at the sound of the familiar voice. The middle aged black man was dressed in sharply creased dark navy woolen pants and a starched long sleeved white cotton shirt. A black bow tie accentuated his outfit and made it clear that his position in the LeBlanc home was one as a servant.

"Thank, you Cyrus. You must have been finished quickly at the general store."

"Yes, Ma'am. I spied you walking in here when they finished loading the last of the coffee, salt, and sugar."

He finished emptying the boxes and stacks of letters and filled the cloth bag almost to the point of overflowing. "Your father sure does like to read, I s'pect."

"That he does," she replied. "I suppose that having trusted friends in Union territory is the only way to keep up with goings on in what is left of our country. He pours over these newspapers from Chicago, New York, and Washington trying to keep abreast of the way the war is progressing."

"Yessum," Cyrus nodded. "But they's must be weeks old by the time we gets 'em down here."

"Sometimes." Her look became somewhat somber as she contemplated the situation in regards to the war. "But he still has a few friends among the steamboat captains that can get up to Saint Louis and Memphis regularly. They pay couriers to mail the newspapers whenever they are close to Confederate held territory."

"I understands, Miss Angelina. Lots of things are harder to get done these days, but Mister Augustin, he always says, where there is a will, there is a way."

"He is ever the optimist." She smiled broadly. "If anyone can find a means to get our cotton crop to market, it would be father." Angelina turned toward the door and nodded as two men entering tipped their hats.

"Morning, Miss," the closer of the two said.

"Morning, gentlemen. It is a fine day we are having."

Her radiant smile was returned by both of the thirty year old bachelors.

Cyrus followed along a few steps behind her—a hint of a smile on his lips. The almost imperceptible shake of his head did not really register with either man, but it was his way of trying to convey that they were wasting their time. Her heart was already taken.

Outside the post office, the redhead turned right along the boardwalk. A platoon of Confederate cavalry rode past in an extended road trot. She stopped for a moment, looking at the enlisted man riding beside the dark haired lieutenant at the head of the column.

Cyrus stopped beside her. "Anybody you know, Miss?"

She shook her head. "No, I was just … "

"Do not you worry your pretty little head of yours. That young man of yours can take care of himself, by all accounts."

"Oh, I do hope so … When I do not hear from him for weeks on end, my confidence wears thin. So many friends have lost brothers, fathers and sons." She turned her head away so as not to give away the exact depth of her anxiety.

"I see how you are … every live long day. I keeps my eyes on you … It is my job, you know. Tell you what … I will go through the mail and if'n I finds a letter from Mister Eric, I be sure to bring it to you over to the bank. You can read it while you waits for your father."

Her eyes sparkled. "I was so hoping that there would be a letter or two from him." She made her way across the bustling street and entered the two story brick building. Angelina spotted a fainting couch with tufted leather upholstery near a window with a view of the street. She pulled her petticoats up behind her knees and took a seat. The twenty year old woman took turns watching the pedestrian traffic on the sidewalk outside and the paneled walnut door to the office of the president of the bank.

Her spirits raised when she saw Cyrus crossing the street with a packet of what appeared to be letters. She leapt to her feet in joyful anticipation.

The head of the LeBlanc household staff grinned from ear to ear as he handed her the missives. There were at least twenty individual letters, all bound with what was once white twine from top to bottom and again from end to end. "Figured you would like to see these, Miss."

"Thank you, Cyrus. You are a gem, indeed."

He departed to wait at the wagon. She tore into the knotted bows binding the twine. Digging into her tiny clutch purse, she produced a small metal nail file to use as a makeshift letter opener. She was so nervous that she missed the gummed flap on the first one two times.

Eagerly, she peaked inside the envelope and removed the folded paper. She hurriedly opened it and began to read the words Eric had written by lantern light.

The bank president's office door opened and her father came out, accompanied by a tall balding man with wire frame glasses. Angelina rose to her feet. She quickly returned the fifth letter she had barely begun reading to its envelope. The men walked directly toward her. Both were grinning.

Augustin LeBlanc was a dark haired wealthy descendant of French aristocracy, whose family had been in the region prior to the Louisiana Purchase.

Tinges of gray streaks were just beginning to appear at his temples, adding to the look of genteel grace.

Unlike many of his contemporary plantation owners, Augustin chose to use free men rather than slaves in his extensive cotton holdings.

"My dear, you do remember Mister Charles Hebert, do you not?"

"Of course, father."

He took hold of her delicate outstretched hand.

"I'm pleased to see you again, sir. How is your lovely wife, Colette?"

"Fine thank you. She is growing weary of the summer heat, but are not we all?"

"Understandably so ... Father, look, I received a packet of letters from Eric." She held up the stack for both men to see.

"Appears he cannot get you out of his mind. I say, you must have made quite an impression on that young major."

She blushed. "Eric has been promoted again, Father ... He is a lieutenant colonel now."

LeBlanc and Hebert exchanged surprised looks. The banker spoke first. "Major Matson introduced Captain Schmidt to me after his glorious victory here over that Yankee cavalry. I knew there was something special about him, even back then."

Augustin laughed. "On that, I believe we all three can agree. But that is not what I came to discuss with Charles. May we step back inside your office?"

"Certainly." He turned and led the way, holding the door for two of his largest depositors.

Once they were all comfortably seated, Augustin began. His face was one of concern. "My dear, we have discussed the potential adverse affects this war is having on world markets for our cotton … Union blockades and the like."

She nodded agreement.

"My concern is twofold … potential threat to your and my livelihood and your ability to handle the LeBlanc holdings if something untoward and unforeseen should happen to me."

"Father, you are still young and healthy … Besides, I took years of tutoring in all the classic disciplines, as you desired."

He held up one finger to his lips. "Permit me to finish, my dear. I've discussed this with Charles, and he has most graciously agreed to teach you something you have not yet learned."

Her forehead furrowed as she tried to imagine whatever that could be.

Hebert grinned. "What your dear father is trying to say, is that I would be most honored to teach you the banking business. He knows farming and marketing, but I can equip you to manage the significant fortune he has amassed in his lifetime."

Angelina sat back in the high-backed leather chair with rows of shiny brass tacks on the armrest supports. "I never heard of a woman banker before."

"Neither have we, but you are certainly bright enough and should be well motivated to learn whatever Charles can present."

She got to her feet, stepped over, and gave Augustin a hug. "Thank you, Father for your faith in me. I shall do my best." She turned to the beaming banker. "Mister Hebert, when may we start?"

§§§

CHAPTER FIVE

SHERMAN, TEXAS

Bass had finished skinning the deer, and had sprinkled salt liberally on the damp fleshy side of the hide. Once it was completely coated to his satisfaction, he folded the legs inside and rolled it up into a tight cylinder—hair side out—and tied it securely with strips of tanned cowhide latigo.

The three heavyset black women working in the freestanding kitchen stepped out to admire his handiwork.

"You gots us nice a one there, Bass. She oughta eat real good."

"Thank you kindly, Miss Martha. "'Spect you is right. Y'all got plenty of fresh vegetables over to the garden. Mind a deer stew would taste mighty fine for supper." He grinned broadly.

She nodded and wiped the flour from her hands on the simple cotton apron. "That's right. You know that's right."

"Best be getting up to the big house and let Massa George know what I gots today. Always likes him some fresh deer backstrap."

"He do," the youngest of the three kitchens slaves replied. "And he say I make the best gravy." She pointed her thumb at herself.

"No such thing!" The oldest black woman, at age thirty five, snapped her kitchen towel as the younger one's backside.

Bass chuckled loudly, his deep voice sounding like distant thunder. "Ain't getting tied up in the middle of all this folderol, no sirree."

He picked up the shotgun, untied the mule and led him to the two story wooden frame house, throwing a clove hitch in Cletus' lead rope on one of the hitching posts outside the whitewashed picket fence.

Bass stepped inside the gate and closed it behind himself, being careful not to let out one of the handful of sheep being employed to keep the lawn surrounding the plantation house neatly trimmed.

As he neared the front door, he heard the sound of riders approaching. Looking over his shoulder, he immediately recognized three members of the Confederate Army.

Huh. Wonder what theys a doin' out this far from town?

He entered the house and began searching for George Reeves. Bass approached Luke, one of the members of the house staff. He pointed over his shoulder. "Company's a coming … Seen Massa George round here?"

The slender young man in a starched white shirt—complete with a black silk string tie—and dark woolen pants pointed down the hall. "Uh huh. He be yonder in the study with his pappy."

"Much obliged." Bass made his way down the hall and tapped on the door frame outside the room filled with books and two ornate desks.

William Steele Reeves, the sixty-two year old patriarch of the wealthy family motioned for him to enter. He was the man who actually owned Bass Reeves, although he had transferred his training and the fruits of his labors over to his son George several years earlier.

"What is it Bass?" the younger man asked.

"Massa George, bagged me that big old doe that I been hearin' 'bout." He held up the shotgun. "One shot … jest like you taught me."

George got to his feet. Bass handed him the weapon and the former Grayson county sheriff and state representative laid it across his desk.

"Good job, boy. Tell Martha the family shall have the pan fried venison steaks tonight." He winked at Bass. "And tell her to save two of 'em for you, as well. You are turning into quite the hunter, if I may say so."

Bass smiled broadly. "Yassah. Thank you, sah. Mighty kind of you." He turned to leave but spun back around. "Y'all want cream gravy with them steaks, doncha?"

"Of course." George chuckled. "Over white rice. That would be very nice, indeed."

Bass nodded. "Uh huh. I let 'em know."

As he passed out the study door, he met Luke leading the three Confederate officers toward the study.

Bass looked them squarely in the eyes and nodded. "Mornin', gentlemens. Fine day we be having ourselves."

The eldest—a Brigadier General wearing the silver stars befitting that rank on his upturned collar—nodded back at the taller black man. "Surely and purely is that. Enjoy it, son."

Luke knocked on the door frame. "Mister Reeves, a General Stephens is here to see Mister George."

William and his son exchanged looks. George shrugged his shoulders, and then shook his head. They both got to their feet as the patriarch motioned for Luke to show them in. The officers entered the study and walked closer to the desks.

Stephens extended his hand to the elder Reeves. "Good to see you again, William."

"Same here, Bobby Don. And who are your fellow soldiers? Don't think I have previously had the honor."

The general stepped to the side. "May I present Major Charles Dickinson and Captain Matthew Pike?" He turned to the two soldiers and motioned with his left hand. "Mister William Steele Reeves and his son, George Robertson Reeves."

The five completed the formal introductions and hand shakes.

William looked out to the hall, where Luke was standing by. "Close the door, if you please."

He did so without another word.

A serious look came over the elder Reeves' face as his brow furrowed. "I take it that this is not a social visit, Bobby Don."

"No, sir. Actually, our business is with your son, but knowing your working relationship here on the plantation, our offer will undoubtedly affect you as well."

Both father and son raised their eyebrows simultaneously as they spoke in unison. "Offer?"

General Stephens smiled. "You both are probably unaware that, as we speak, a large force of the Army of Virginia is engaged in a pitch battle with forces of the Union Army near a place called Gettysburg, Pennsylvania ... never heard of it before and had to look it up on the map myself ... It seems General Lee decided to force the Union's hand. Heretofore, Mister Lincoln's General McClellen was quite reluctant to engage him in a major battle with his Army of the Potomac."

George was astounded by the news. "Pennsylvania? That would mean that Lee's forces have circled north of Washington. They could be in a position to defeat the Union Armies protecting the capitol. That could possibly bring these prolonged unpleasantries to a negotiated settlement."

A huge grin came across the general's face. He turned to his subordinates. "See, men? What did I tell you about George Reeves? He recognized the importance of Lee's strategic plan immediately."

Both junior officers nodded.

George raised his eyebrows. "Gentlemen, you perhaps give me far to much credit ... I merely observed an obvious possibility from such a maneuver. As you are undoubtedly aware, I have no military background in any fashion."

"Absolutely, Mister Reeves. I am well acquainted with your background. What I do know is that you possess a superior intellect, a sharp sense of civic duty and have gained the respect of many in the legislature down in Austin."

General Stephens' brown eyes narrowed. "Sir, I will cut to the chase. We have formed another brigade of Texas volunteers to help support General Lee back east. I, sir, am in dire need of a man who can lead a company of these troops into battle. You may or may not be aware, but our forces choose their own leaders. My men have chosen you."

George gasped slightly. "Sir, I am truly honored." Suddenly, he found his mouth was unexpectedly dry.

He took a sip of water from a cut crystal glass, and then glanced over at his father.

William's brow was furrowed. "Son, do not worry about me for a second. I shall have one of your brothers fill in for you here until you return. Do your duty and see what you can accomplish to win this War of Northern Aggression."

George tossed back the rest of the water and set the glass down on his desk. "General, if Texas and the Confederacy need me, how could I ever refuse?" He stood up straight and extended his hand. "At your service, sir."

General Stephens shook it firmly. "Welcome aboard, Captain Reeves."

Major Dickinson and Captain Pike came to attention, clicking their heels together on the polished heart of pine floors. They snapped crisp salutes to the newly commissioned officer.

George tried his best to return the gesture, but his eyes strayed to the angle of his hand and then back to their more correct versions. "I think you boys will have your work cut out with some of this military stuff."

The others laughed …

After lunch, the three officers in uniform tightened the girths on their mounts as George kissed his wife Jane and nine children farewell on the porch.

Bass Reeves stood by hitching posts, holding the reins to his new mount—a sorrel Morgan gelding fitted with a high backed saddle and a pair of stuffed saddlebags.

Tied up next to him was George's ash gray gelding.

He waved at the fifteen or so colored folk who had gathered to watch the momentous departure. Several had tears in their eyes as they contemplated the imminent departure of their friend and had concerns about his safety.

George lowered the smallest of his offspring down to the porch, forced a smile, and said, "Papa will be back before you know it. Mind your mother … and keep me in your prayers." His eyes misted over.

He turned and walked quickly down the steps and strode across the yard with a quickness in his step. The newly commissioned major passed though the gate in the picket fence and secured it closed.

The three other Confederate officers had already mounted up. Bass unhitched the lead rope to the gray and handed it to his master. "Here you go, Massa."

George nodded and laid the rope across his horse's neck under the reins before he swung into the saddle.

Bass forked his saddle and squirmed a bit, trying to find a comfortable position in the different rig than he was accustomed to using.

General Stephens led out with the others in trail. Captain Reeves squeezed the gray into a little faster trot to come up alongside.

"What is the first order of business, General?"

Bobby Don smiled. "My plan is get you introduced to the men of your company. Then one of them will see that you get over to the quartermasters for a uniform fitting, get your sidearms issued, and finally ... a tent large enough for you and your man servant."

"I take it that you will be tied up with more pressing matters, is that correct?"

"Unfortunately, your assumption is correct. We have training scheduled for most of the afternoon, but after the evening mess ... supper in civilian terms ... we should be able to sit down, get ourselves more acquainted, and discuss the logistics of getting this conglomeration of Texas Volunteers back east where we can do some serious fighting."

George nodded and considered how much he had to learn in a short time. "Sounds reasonable to me, sir." He nodded and wheeled his mount around to pull up beside Bass.

"How are you and Whiskey getting along?"

"Well, sir, me and Whiskey is just now gettin' to know one another. He seems like he got a lot of spirit to him. I wuz kinda taken by surprise when you said you did not want me to ride my old mule."

George grinned. "To tell you the truth, I did not think Cletus had three thousand miles in him."

Bass' eyes grew wide as saucers. "Three thousand miles? We going three thousand miles?"

His master laughed. "Not in one direction. It is fifteen hundred miles there … and fifteen hundred back."

Bass let out a low whistle. "Whoo weee. I ain't never rode that far in all my born days."

"It will take us a while, I reckon. Besides, I liked the idea of having Whiskey as a back up in case ol' Dollar here gets shot."

A look of concern crossed Bass' face. "Shot? They shoot horses in that war y'all been a talking 'bout?"

"'Fraid so," George said as the smile left his face. "War is a serious business. It is not all flags and parades, I can tell you that."

Bass nodded, not understanding or particularly liking what he had heard so far. *I 'spect this will be differn't than what I know. Better keep my eyes and ears open and my mouth shut.*

§§§

CHAPTER SIX

ARKANSAS RIVER BOTTOM

The column of Confederate cavalry approached the ferry crossing ninety miles southeast of Little Rock. Union Major Oliver Winthorpe rode beside the rebel colonel who held him and the other train derailment survivors captive.

He stared in the distance and could distinctly make out the blue uniforms of the Union soldiers guarding the ferry.

He took a side look at the younger commander, and then back at the soldiers posted by the slow moving river. *Surely he can see the crossing is guarded. I cannot believe he did not send scouts ahead to ascertain the tactical situation.*

He looked back at the blond headed Confederate.

Tiny lines around the young Texan's eyes gave away the game. The bushy blond mustache covered the smile that he was attempting to suppress. "What is wrong Oliver? See something that has you slightly confused?"

The career army man let out a sigh. "Tarnation, son. You have picked up rather quickly in the art of deception. Learn that from that Chinese philosopher as well?"

"Perhaps a little, but my father taught me how to make decoys for ducks when I was a kid. Mind you, they were not exact replicas, but the mallards and pintails did not seem to figure that out until they were in range."

"By then it was too late."

"Right you are, sir. As you will see in a minute or two, the original Union security detail was taken by surprise, and my boys borrowed their uniforms for a couple of days."

He held up a gloved hand. "And before you recite the penalty for being a spy or some such thing, may I point out that Arkansas seceded from the Union as well, and therefore, this is technically not enemy territory for my men."

Winthorpe signed and nodded. "Always one step ahead."

"I try my best."

Twenty minutes later the last of the confederate wagons had made the short trip across the river. A pair of rebel scouts from the southwest approached the military convoy. They spotted Lieutenant Colonel Schmidt and rode up to give their report.

"Colonel, Sergeant Watson, reporting as ordered."

"Very well, Billy. Any major changes in union patrols since we passed through their lines four days ago?"

"Nary a bit, sir. They's way too few of 'em to make a decent front. Since our boys to the south was ordered not to engage 'em until they get the word, them Yanks seem to be gettin' a mite lax."

Eric took in the information and pondered a bit. "I figure we have at least a two day head start on the Union forces out of Little Rock. They will not know for certain our final direction of travel since we plan to veer back to the west in about ten miles."

Captain Ingrham spoke up. "Colonel, did you decide if you wanted us to destroy the ferry or not?"

Colonel Schmidt shook his head. "Doran, I think the locals here would be downright disgusted with us if we were to do that. There is not another decent river crossing between here and Pine Bluff."

He thumbed south toward the largest town within sixty miles. "The Yanks are unlikely to pose any threat to our withdrawal in the next ten hours. Once we get back across our lines, they will not be able to mount a serious attack, in any event. Pass the word to leave it intact."

Ingrham winked and gave the colonel a nod. "You got it. Will catch up with you." He wheeled about, and carried out his orders.

Eric turned back to his scout. "Got another job for you as well, Billy. Get back down to our encampment near Tulip. Advise Colonel Dobbins of our intention to camp with his cavalry detachment overnight. He will undoubtedly be pleased to hear that we have captured a significant amount of victuals and are more than happy to share."

"Yes, sir! Archie will appreciate them, that is for sure. I will try to find us a nice spot to make camp while I'm at it."

The colonel grinned. "God speed, Billy. We will see you 'bout supper time."

Major Winthorpe watched as the enlisted cavalryman urged his pony into a road trot and began to distance himself from the convoy. "If I may say so, Colonel, it appears that you have a good man there."

"Take that as a compliment on his behalf. My men are quite capable of not only carrying out my orders, but operating independently if the need arises. I do not choose to make myself indispensable."

"I see … note that you and your men have dispensed with many of the military customs of a uniformed force. For example, your Captain Ingrham and that sergeant you called Billy did not salute you when they left your presence."

Eric laughed heartily. "Could see that that bothered you. Tiny little facial expressions, a slight squint of your eyes, that sort of thing … You do not play poker by any chance?"

The Union major was somewhat taken aback by the question. His back stiffened slightly. "My Christian denomination denounces gambling."

"I understand … A result of their perception the Roman soldiers casting lots for Christ's clothes at the crucifixion, no doubt."

"Believe you are correct. But what has that to do with my playing cards?"

"My fellow officers … at least those I count as friends … who have attempted to teach me the art of playing poker have emphasized that I learn to read an opponent's face. Most players, but not all by any means, give what they refer to as a *tell*. Sometimes they are signaling when they have a strong hand … other times it merely means that they are bluffing."

Eric grinned. "That, of course is a gentleman's way of saying that they are lying about their position in hopes to dissuade you to give up prematurely."

The major mulled over the concept for a few seconds. "In some ways, the art of war could find parallels in your game of cards."

"True. A battle won by deception has fewer casualties than one in which wholesale bloodletting determines the survivor, and in turn, the so-called victor."

Eric leaned a little closer the Union officer.. "To return to the earlier part of the conversation, I shall let you in on a little secret."

Winthorpe's eyebrows rose at the mention of that word.

"Unless we are in a secure Confederate encampment, I have directed my men not to salute me or other senior officers. We both know that Union forces possess telescopes, and binoculars that can observe us quite clearly from a distance. Our uniform rank insignia may not be visible, but I feel that a salute is all the proof that a capable sniper needs to engage a stationary, high value target. I have done so myself on numerous occasions."

Eric smiled and let that last sentence sink in, noting as the major swallowed.

"In light of that unfortunate potentiality, we determined that slight modifications of the rules of military decorum were in order."

Winthorpe nodded. "I had heard some of our general officers wore the outer garments of an enlisted private for just such a reason."

"A Sharp's rifle in the hands of a capable marksman can take out a man at a half mile." Eric's eyes drifted forward along the route that the convoy was taking. He scanned the scattered woods that dotted the ridges and creek bottoms.

As the sun drooped halfway toward the western horizon, the convoy came across the main road between Pine Bluff and Tulip.

A scout rode down from a wooded hillside and made his report. "Corporal Simpson reporting all clear to the west, sir. They be a passle of Yanks back east over to Pine Bluff, but they seem to want to stick close to the town, mostly."

"That's about twenty five miles from here?" Schmidt asked.

"Yessir. I sent one of the boys to set up an observation post off the road 'bout ten miles from here. He had a good line of sight for another five miles, just in case they decided to venture out thisaway."

"Good job, Bobby. I would like for you to retrieve your scout and join up with us in Tulip tonight. We shall let the First Arkansas Cavalry provide our rear flank security from this point."

"As you wish, Colonel." He looked at the size of the convoy and all the Union prisoners. "Looks like y'all done good up north."

Eric nodded. "Our casualties were appreciably lower than expected. Picked up a significant contingent of prisoners and some much needed rations. Assuming we make it to our destination without further incident, this will be regarded as a successful mission."

The young corporal tipped his hat. "See y'all in camp then. The road is a good one all the way to town." He reined about and set off to the east at a fast walk.

The terrain around Tulip, Arkansas, was predominantly engaged in the production of cotton. Wide fields lined the road on both sides, with thigh high plants filling the rows. The blazing summer sun beat down on the expansive plantations. A group of over a dozen slaves, clad in homespun white cotton garments, rhythmically chopped at the weeds attempting to take hold in the rich black soil between the rows. They sang an old Negro spiritual about Joshua at the battle of Jericho.

A white overseer rode a chestnut mare and carried a double barreled shotgun across his lap. He waved at the convoy, and many soldiers returned the gesture.

In the distance, a white two story house dominated the landscape. It had a Greek revival architecture, complete with Corinthian capped columns across the front porch. It was surrounded by acres of gardens, a barn, corrals, and numerous small, and larger outbuildings.

Winthorpe took in the sight. "You know, this is this first time I ever saw a real plantation."

Eric nodded. "This town we are destined for is called Tulip. It came close to being voted capital of Arkansas."

"You don't say … is cotton its source wealth and fame?"

"Not by a long shot. It is mostly famous as a center of higher education. They call themselves the Athens of Arkansas."

"Do not recall that I ever heard of that. What schools are here?"

"The Methodist Church founded one for women called the Tulip Female Collegiate Seminary and there was an Arkansas Military Institute, but I am told they disbanded after the faculty and staff was mustered into the Confederate Army en masse."

"Really." Winthorpe studied a field hand for a few seconds. He eyes narrowed at the sight of the white overseer. "Tell me ... are those workers that we see in the fields all slaves?"

"Suppose they are. Would not need an overseer with a shotgun to keep you working if you are getting paid."

"But President Lincoln freed the slaves back in January of last year."

Eric burst out laughing. "The Emancipation Proclamation? Now that is funny ... you do know that the proclamation only freed slaves in states that no longer recognize federal sovereignty? If your Mister Lincoln is such a staunch opponent of slavery, why did he not free the slaves in the north as well?"

The major was perplexed for a moment. "Perhaps he did not wish to disrupt the status quo among slave holders in the north during this conflict."

"Are you referring to your General Ulysses S. Grant? I understand that he keeps slaves while our Robert E. Lee freed his." The young Colonel grinned. "Those are merely a couple of the many things that do not quite add up about this conflict. When looked at it from our Southern perspective, it would appear that Mister Lincoln desired to create an uprising among the slaves in the states of the Confederacy."

Eric rolled his shoulders to shake off an imminent cramp in his trapezoids. "To me, that Emancipation Proclamation is as transparent as it can be. Lincoln overlooked the fact that many slaves cannot read or write, and their literate masters had nothing to gain by spreading the news of that obnoxious and impotent missive."

The major stared at the younger man for a moment, lost for words. "Every time we discuss this unfortunate war between the states of the Union, I seem to become more and more uncertain of the motives behind it."

Eric nodded. "On that, sir, we can agree. I tend to try to relate the South's secession to a marital union. One party did not feel they were being properly respected and no longer wished to remain in the union. They took legal action to secure a divorce. The problem arose when the other party refused to move out of the house that no longer belonged to them."

He locked eyes with Major Winthorpe. He could tell the wheels were turning as his prisoner contemplated that simple analogy.

After a few seconds, the major replied, "Never quite heard it put that way, but I will be danged if I can find much fault to it." He looked away and stared into the distance.

Eric waited for a few seconds before continuing. "I have read the text of speeches your President made in defense of his willingness to initiate hostilities against the Confederacy. On the surface, the words seem well reasoned and patriotic to the importance of the intellectual concept of truly United States ... I only wish he had found his voice years earlier and set it to the task of finding a means to insure domestic tax policies were equitable for all states."

He took a look back over his shoulder at the field hands chopping weeds in the distance and sighed before he took in a deep breath.

"The issue of slavery has dogged your *United States* since its conception. It almost derailed the Continental Congress, and only by its inclusion would the southern states agree to join ... I wonder how things would have worked out if that Union commander in South Carolina would have turned over the fort to the rightful owners as they did in all the other states? Would Lincoln have declared war on us under those circumstances? Could the two nations have coexisted side by side?"

§§§

CHAPTER SEVEN

LEBLANC PLANTATION

At the edge of 3,000 acres of cotton fields abutting the Red River south of Shreveport, Louisiana stood a majestic French style chateau. A private road lined with mature red oak trees provided a canopy of shade for most of the year as it wound past the road to the warehouses, smokehouse, employee housing, the six acre garden, and stables.

In numerous paddocks, the plantation's Standardbred and Tennessee Walking horses milled about. Farther away from the house were more paddocks for the operation's draft horses and mules.

Surrounding the six thousand square foot house—a magnificent example of French Empire design, complete with mansard roof—were well manicured lawns kept short by a small flock of grazing sheep.

Angelina LeBlanc sat comfortably in a caned bottomed rocking chair, rereading the stack of letters from the dashing young Confederate officer who had won her heart.

Augustin glanced out the leaded glass doors leading to the sixty foot wide porch and grinned. The dark haired cotton magnate noted the huge smile come upon her face. It reminded him so much of his dearly departed wife that he had to look away for a second.

His eyes fell upon the huge life-sized oil painting of Elouise LeBlanc prominently displayed on the mantle above the elegantly carved marble fireplace. "Oh, *mon amor*, if you could only see our little girl all grown up."

Tears briefly rimmed his eyes, but he blinked, and then smiled at the sight of his daughter so happy. The tears disappeared by the time he turned the polished brass handle on the door to the porch.

He stepped out on to the slate gray bricks laid in a herringbone pattern and silently closed the door behind him. "My dear, are you planning to wear those letters completely out? How many times have you read them through?"

Angelina rocked back and shot him a side glance over her right shoulder. "Father, do not be silly. One cannot wear a letter out in two days. Besides, there were eleven of them in this bundle." She smiled broadly.

"That is what Cyrus told me. I am pleased to note your young man had not forgotten you."

"I certainly do not foresee that as a possibility."

Augustin grinned. "Neither do I … I like your young man. He has depth."

"And he is brilliant and brave and … "

"Handsome and kind … Believe I have heard all of those before." He chuckled.

She burst into laughter. "Touché, Monsieur LeBlanc. Am I being overly infatuated with him? I never felt this way before with any other man."

"Not at all … Eric has some wonderful qualities. He is very bright." Augustin's smile faded to a more somber look. "I do worry about his safety, though. Life in the cavalry is hard and quite dangerous."

Lines furrowed her forehead. "But we will still pray for him every day, will we not?"

He reached out and tousled her hair ever so gently. "That we will, my dear, that we will. God is all powerful, and if it is His desire, Eric will come back to you safe and sound."

Angelina rose to her feet, threw her arms around her father, and hugged him very hard.

SHERMAN, TEXAS

Bass Reeves waited patiently outside the dressing room in the small tailor's shop. After a few minutes, his master, George Reeves, walked out, wearing the wool uniform of a captain in the cavalry of the Confederacy.

The cadet gray shell coat had a single row of nine shiny brass buttons, an upright collar with a single woven-wire gold star on each side, and a thin Austrian braided knot embroidered on both sleeves. At the cuff, adjacent to the knot was a sizable chevron of yellow material denoting the branch of service of the wearer.

His pants, a light blue wool with a contrasting one and a half inch wide stripe of a yellow cotton cloth, folded over themselves atop his newly issued cavalry boots.

He carried his yellow kepi in his hand and stepped onto the rectangular wooden platform in front of three mirrors. George looked himself up and down and tugged the headgear into place.

He frowned and muttered, "I am afraid this will never do." The newly minted officer tugged at the sides of his coat. "This is a big as a house."

The smallish tailor stepped to his side and smiled. "They all say that." He handed George a black leather belt with an oval buckle. The letters *CS* were cast into the face.

On the left side hung an officer's saber in a shiny nickel plated brass scabbard. "Put this on and you shall see what I mean."

Reeves shot the man a disbelieving glance but wrapped the belt around his waist and snugged it tight, looping the excess through the right side of the buckle and securing the single hook into one of the many pre-punched holes.

He adjusted the saber to where it felt comfortable at his side. Looking in the mirrors, he could see much of the excess material was then not as apparent, but still was not pleased at the sight of what he perceived as a baggy fit.

"Now sir ... Draw your saber, if you would be so kind." The tailor chuckled.

George grasped the scabbard and withdrew the wicked blade with a slight hiss. He held the tip upright, and then quickly pointed it at the mirror as if to signal a charge.

Bass' eyes grew wide at the first sight of his master in a military officer's uniform.

"Tell me, sir ... does the tunic bind you or inhibit your movement at all?"

The captain contemplated the question for a moment. "No ... I cannot say that it does."

The tailor smiled broadly. "Then, sir, I must advise you that the uniform ... at least the blouse, is a perfect fit. The adventure upon which you are about to embark is not the place for a Beau Brummell. Without a doubt, I could make the coat fit like the veritable glove, but I would be quite remiss in doing so. The profession of arms is a challenging one, I assure you."

George quickly mulled over what the tailor had said. He sheathed the saber. It locked into place with a slight click. "I thank you, kind sir, for your wise council. Now, then, if we may attend to the hem of these pants."

The tailor quickly stepped in with a small pin cushion fastened to his left wrist. With movements attesting to his years at the craft, he folded the excess material up and under and pinned one pant leg in place.

He then took a small sliver of soap and made a mark on the bottom where the proper hem should rest. "Please step back into the dressing room and remove these. I shall have them ready shortly."

"That sounds wonderful." He turned to his man servant. "Bass, come with me. I may need some help with the new boots. Oh, I want you to fold up my civilian clothes neatly. I am certain this establishment has some wrapping paper and twine with which to tie them up in a tidy bundle … I shall not be needing them for some time."

Bass nodded. "Yassah. I can do that."

Twenty minutes later, George and Bass departed the tailor shop. The muscular black slave carried the bundled clothes under his right arm and two slightly worn riding boots in his left hand.

When they reached their mounts, Bass busied himself with tying the civilian clothes to the back of his saddle and folded the boots to fit inside his saddlebag.

George fished inside his pants for a pair of silver dollars and then handed them to Bass. "Tonight is our last night in Sherman. The Colonel told me that we leave for Louisiana on the morning train." He pointed across the street a half block.

"Go down to that mercantile and pick me up two jugs of good whiskey. I wish to have a little get together with my officers and senior enlisted personnel tonight."

The news took Bass by surprise. The replacement cavalry unit had only been together for a few days, and his master still did not have all the men's names committed to memory.

"Yassah, Massa ... uh ... Am I ... uh ... Am I supposed to call you Massa or Captain now that you be all dressed up in that there ..." He motioned to George's new attire with his thumb.

"Uniform, Bass. This ensemble is called a military uniform." He grinned as he pointed at his new jacket with both hands. "I suppose that it would be more fitting and proper if you referred to me as Captain Reeves."

Bass nodded. "Yassah. I tries to do that."

George tightened his horse's girth, and then untied the lead rope from the hitching post. He hopped up, stabbed his new boot inside the stirrup, and swung into the saddle. "Meet me back in camp. I have a few important things to take care of before we depart."

"You can count on me, Captain. Be there directly."

The major backed his horse away from the rail, wheeled it about, and nudged it into a slow trot. A pair of Confederate enlisted cavalry rode passed and saluted him. He returned the gesture and quickly disappeared among a crowd of riders in the busy town.

Bass saddled up and worked his way through the traffic, finding an empty spot along the peeled pine hitching rail.

He dismounted and tied up his horse with the lead rope. He left it long enough where the steed could reach the cypress water trough placed beneath it. "Git you somethin' to drink, Whiskey. Ol' Bass will be back out in a minute or two." He patted the sorrel on the neck.

He walked around the hitching post and stepped up on the sawn plank boardwalk. Bass looked inside the storefront windows and marveled at the stacks of canned goods and utensils on display. Above the entrance hung a large wooden sign with the establishment's name painted in black letters.

WITHERSPOON

MERCANTILE

The sign meant nothing to him as he could not read. He tipped his hat to a pair of forty year old women who were leaving and made his way passed them through the door.

It took him a moment for his eyes to adjust from the bright Texas sun outside on the street. He looked on with wonder at the varied array of products. The big man had never had been allowed to shop unaccompanied, as he never had any money of his own.

He walked up and down the five rows but saw nothing that looked like what he was seeking. Bass made his way to the counter on the side wall near the front.

Glass jars filled with penny candy of all sorts were prominently displayed on the well worn wood countertop. Behind it, a gray haired clerk was unpacking a case of canned peaches. Bass removed his flat brimmed hat and held it across his chest. "Scuse me there, sir."

The old man cast a somewhat jaundiced eye upon him. "What is you want, boy?"

Bass looked him straight in the eye. "My massa sent me in here to buys some whiskey fo' him and the mens in his company."

"And what company would that be? I know most of the businesses here in town, but I do not recall having seen you before."

"Nawsah." Bass shook his head. "Ain't never been in here 'afor today. I works out on the farm, mostly."

"I see. Now what was the name of the company?"

The big black man's face screwed up as he tried to think of an easy explanation. "Well, sah. He work for a Colonel and a General … Don't rightly know they names. His company has a number, fo' sho."

"Oh, your master is in the army."

Bass shook his head. "Not 'xactly … Mind they calls it the calvary."

The shopkeeper broke into a grin. *My God, if this goober does not beat all. Poor colored boy does not know nothin' about nothin'. It is a pure dee wonder he can dress himself.* He leaned closer. "Rye or Kentucky Bourbon?"

Bass shrugged and scratched his head. "Cain't say."

The clerk's jaw dropped. "If you cannot say, who can? What does the man drink?"

"He say to get two jugs of good whiskey. I ain't never tasted neither of them you said."

"Mother of God", the old man muttered. "How much money did he give you?"

Bass slapped the two silver dollars on the counter.

"Now we are gettin' somewhere. Did you bring your own jugs?"

Bass shook his head vigorously. "Nawsah. We did not bring none with us when we rode out."

"Somehow, I expected that." The clerk stepped to his left a few feet and pulled out a pair of dark brown glazed pottery jugs with cork stoppers. They had circular ridges around the circumference to enhance the design that resembled a beehive.

Each had a single heavy finger loop in the neck for holding the precious cargo. "Wait right here. I shall fill these and be back."

"Yassah," Bass said as he breathed a sigh of relief. *I never knowed is was gonna be so hard jest to buy somethin'.*

The clerk made his way to the storeroom where several heavy oaken barrels were stacked against the wall. Two were mounted in sturdy purpose-built cradles to allow the barrels to lie on their sides.

A wooden spigot was hammered tightly into the bung hold on each barrel top. He carefully filled one jug from a cask marked *Rye Whiskey*. Catching the last drop of the amber liquid on his finger he bought it to his lips and ran his tongue across them. *Nectar of the Gods, it truly is.*

The second barrel was marked *Jim Beam Kentucky Bourbon*. He filled the remaining jug and capped it off by smartly smacking the cork home. When he got back to the counter, he spotted Bass with his nose to the canisters of penny candy. He sat the heavy containers down. "Like what you see?"

Bass nodded. "They all be different colors. Some look like little crystal rocks, and some have red stripes, others have black stripes." He pointed at a jar half filled with cinnamon flavored rock candy. "These here are just red like blood. What they for?"

"Never had penny candy before?" The clerk was incredulous.

"Ain't never had me no penny. Massa Reeves, he jest gives me food, clothes, and a roof over my head."

The clerk simply sighed. *That there is some kind of pitiful.* He tried not to feel sorry for Bass but it didn't work. He got out a small tally book and began to record the sale. "One gallon rye whiskey - three bits. One gallon of Jim Beam - four bits." He glanced over his wire rimmed glasses. "Ever since those yahoos in Richmond outlawed the distillation of corn into whiskey, the price keeps goin' up. I'm down to my last three barrels of bourbon. When they are gone, that is the end of the hunt."

Bass nodded as if he understood. He had never heard of Richmond before.

"Two gallon jugs … ten cents apiece."

"How much do that all come to? Did the Captain give me enough money?"

The clerk swallowed at the lump that was unexpectedly starting to grow in his throat. "Total comes to a buck ninety five … I owe you a nickel."

Bass looked relieved.

The clerk took in a deep breath. "Tell you what. The hard candy is four for a penny. That means you can get twenty pieces for that nickel. Aw, hell, make it twenty-five. I will make up your receipt to show an even two dollars."

Bass was not sure. He had never tasted any hard candy. The temptation was very high. He shook his head slowly. "Better not. My massa might not like …"

The old man cut him off. "Son, the Captain has bigger fish to fry. I hear tell you boys are bound off to fight the war back east … That nickel difference is not gonna mean a tinker's damn, if you pardon my French. And you …"

He pointed his index finger at the much larger man. "… like it or not, you are goin' to be in the thick of things."

It was Bass' turn to swallow. He could tell looking at the old man's blue eyes that he was serious. "Which ones should I get?"

"How 'bout if'n I pick out an assortment for you? I will tell you what they are called ... you can decide if you like them. That way, the next time you come in, you can pick out your favorite." He winked and nodded.

"I s'pose that be the best thing to do."

The man got a small brown paper bag and lifted up the glass top on the closest canister. "These are plain rock candy. I sell a lot of 'em."

He took two and dropped them in the sack. Placing the glass lid carefully back in place, he moved to the next one. "Peppermint sticks ... another favorite."

He grabbed one and handed it to Bass. "Take a lick. These travel well ... as long as you keep 'em dry."

Bass complied. His eyes grew wide. "Good gosh! It kinda tastes like a mint leaf with cracked black pepper on it! Only stronger ... And it is sweeter than honey."

The clerk grinned. "Suppose you could say that. You can keep that one out if you like."

Bass nodded and lolled the stick around in his mouth , savoring the new taste sensation.

"Now this black and white striped one is a called a hoarshound. You might find it a little bitter, but it is really good for a sore throat."

After a few minutes, Bass had also been introduced to Jordan Almonds (his favorite), Turkish delights—a hot cinnamon rock candy—and a rolled hard candy called Neccos. He tucked the sack inside his bib overalls.

The clerk reached over, picked up the two silver dollars and pushed the two gallon jugs of whiskey toward the black man.

Bass started to reach for the handle but stopped. He looked at the old man. "Mister, you been real nice and helpful ... seein' as how this was my first time shoppin' by myself and all. Can I ask you somethin'?"

"Sure. I suppose so."

"What is your name? I wants to remember you while I be gone off to war with Captain Reeves and them."

The clerk suddenly felt that lump return to his throat. "Farmer ... My name is Ken Farmer."

Bass stuck out his hand. "They calls me Bass Reeves. I be much pleased to meet you, sir."

Ken took his hand firmly and the two men locked eyes. "Pleased to meet you, Bass. May God guide and protect you on your journey."

Bass nodded and released his handshake. "Well, sir, I best be on my way a'fore the Captain goes to wonderin' where I be." He grabbed the two jugs and headed for the door.

Farmer slipped off his glasses. He lifted up the bottom corner of his white cotton shop apron and dabbed away a couple of tears.

Once he had secured one jug in a saddle bag and tied the second one on tightly with a length of latigo, Bass unhitched the gelding's lead rope and mounted up.

He reined east toward the Confederate camp and leaned over as he patted the sorrel's neck. "Whiskey, you ain't gonna believe this ... I just met me a white man that prayed for me. Ain't that somethin'?"

§§§

CHAPTER EIGHT

ARKADELPHIA, ARKANSAS

It was almost noon when the convoy of captured Union soldiers and provisions reached the Confederate regional headquarters stockade compound built on the outskirts of the small town.

The guards swung the front gates open as Lt. Colonel Eric Schmidt led the column inside with the Union major riding alongside. An entire company of infantry assigned to temporarily guard the prisoners was dispatched on either side of the column, their rifles carried at port arms, ready to engage in an instant.

A rebel major stood outside a small wood framed private home, converted to an office and residence for the camp. He saluted as the convoy came to a halt. "Afternoon, Colonel. May I commend you and your men on a most successful mission."

Eric and the Union officer returned the salute and dismounted. The lanky Texan removed his riding gloves and reached for the outstretched hand of his fellow officer. "Appreciate it, Billy. It went pretty much according to plan, for once ... May I introduce Major Oliver Winthorpe? He is the ranking officer of the prisoners of war."

The Confederate major shook hands with his counterpart. "How do you do, sir? Major Billy Whitfield, at your service. Understand you were with the Fourteenth Infantry Battalion."

Oliver's face gave up the surprise that his former unit's designation was already known to his captor's distant headquarters. "Why, yes, that is correct."

Eric didn't miss the tiny detail. He leaned in closer to Winthorpe and simply whispered, "Dispatches." He grinned.

"You southern boys do not let the grass grow beneath your feet, now, do you?"

Major Whitfield laughed. "We do make a passable attempt to try to keep up ... Certainly, Colonel Schmidt advised you of the penalties for attempting to escape. For you and your men ... the war is over."

He pointed at the rough sawn slabs of virgin Arkansas pine fashioned into a formidable barrier. "I would be remiss not to point out the ten foot tall fences surrounding this compound. These guards are excellent marksmen and equipped with some of the finest rifles and scatterguns ever made."

His smile faded to a continence of deadly seriousness. "Neither of us would like to see your young men martyred in a vain attempt to escape capture. We have a converted tobacco drying shed as a temporary shelter for your troops. Our doctor will make regular rounds to tend to your wounded, but we plan to move you to a prisoner camp in Texas in the very near future."

The union officer nodded. "Colonel Schmidt and I discussed that possibility on the way here. I will address my troops and request that they make no foolish attempts at a break out. You Confederates have been more than hospitable, considering the most unfortunate of circumstances."

Eric turned to Major Winthorpe and extended his hand. "Sir, it has been a distinct pleasure making your acquaintance. Hope that after these hostilities have ended we can meet again one day, as friends."

A slight smile came to the major's face as he shook the young colonel's hand firmly. "That, sir, would please me as well. May God be with you and keep you safe."

"And may his many blessings fall upon you, as well." Eric released the man's grasp, came to attention, and snapped a crisp salute. He wheeled around, grabbed the reins of his black stallion, and swung effortlessly into the saddle.

"Major Ingrham. Take charge of the battalion. See that a large proportion of the spoils are distributed to the quartermaster. I shall head over to headquarters to inquire on our next orders."

"Aye, sir. As you wish." Doran began passing orders though his subordinates to carry out the directives.

Eric rode up to the main gate, and the four sentries opened it up to let him pass. He turned west down Walnut Street, and brought Thunder up to a road trot. "Bet it feels good to stretch out those long legs of yours, big boy."

Coming to the intersection of Third Street, he turned north and headed toward the downtown section. He passed a number of frame houses, and two churches, one Baptist and the other a Methodist.

After several minutes, he arrived at the site of the former Arkadelphia Institute. A two story wooden structure, the school served as both a high school and college seminary that had been built only thirteen years before by a Baptist representative of the American Bible Society.

Following the outbreak of the War Between the States, most of the male students enlisted in the Confederacy or were drafted — the school closed soon thereafter. A sign placed on the lawn had been painted over with the words

NO TIME TO DIE

CSA
HEADQUARTERS

Eric pulled up alongside a long peeled pine hitching rail. Several other horses with *CSA* branded on them were already tied there. He found a spot that gave the black stallion a little extra space between him and the adjoining mounts.

He swung down and tied off the lead rope before he loosened the girth a couple of notches. "Behave yourself, Thunder. You have nothing to prove with these other ponies." He patted the spirited steed on the neck.

Thunder whinnied and shook his head as if he understood.

Two enlisted men, one a private and the other a corporal, stood guard duty under the shade of a cupola located at the front of the headquarters. They came to attention and brought their rifles to *present arms* as the lieutenant colonel strode up the sidewalk.

Eric folded his riding gloves and tucked them under his gun belt. He snapped a salute to the guards. "Afternoon, gents. Is General Briley in, by any chance?"

"Yes, sir," the corporal replied. "He and the staff are in a meeting, as I understand."

"Thank you ... As you were."

The enlisted men moved back through the positions of *port arms* and *order arms*. One of them reached for the front door handle and held it open for the young officer.

Well disciplined and trained. Good sign. Eric removed his cavalry hat, beating some of the road dust off the sweat-stained headgear before he stepped inside.

A clean shaven master sergeant seated at a desk near the entrance recognized him as he entered. He rose to his feet as he grinned. "Welcome back, Colonel. Bully good show on the Yankee railway operation! General Briley was most pleased with the reports."

"Was happy myself that we did not lose more men. The captured provisions will come in handy. Of that, I am certain."

"You are correct, sir. The General and his staff are discussing some major strategic plans ... in light of the recent major setbacks."

The affable young officer's eyebrows raised. "Setbacks?"

The master sergeant's face took on a more somber countenance. "Best I let the General fill you in, sir. It happened after you departed on this last mission. We just found out about it ourselves two days ago."

Eric took in the news and looked up the stairwell. "They are in his office I take it?"

"Yes, sir. They have been expecting you."

Schmidt took to the stairs with a purpose, his saber swaying off his left hip. Arriving at the second floor, he turned left to the last classroom at the end of the hall.

It made a spacious office for the Division Commander. It had windows on two exterior walls and two blackboards on each of the interiors ones. A hand painted pecan wood plaque was affixed to the closed hallway door.

CHAD BRILEY
MAJOR GENERAL
CSA

Eric knocked twice and entered. Six officers were gathered around a desk with a stack of maps rolled out upon it, and they all looked up at the tall man coming inside to join them.

He made eye contact with the shorter and slightly portly major general. "Lieutenant Colonel Eric Schmidt reporting as ordered, sir." He snapped a crisp salute.

Briley returned the salute, and then extended his hand. "Hell of a job, son. Hell of a job ... At least we have some bright spots to discuss."

Eric nodded. "Your sergeant downstairs mentioned some type of recent setback. May I be so bold as to inquire about the nature of such a calamity?"

Briley shook his head. "Son, you yourself predicted as much before you departed ... Vicksburg fell. Half of the whole damn Confederate Army of Mississippi surrendered on the fourth of July."

Schmidt took in a deep breath and let it out slowly. He glanced at the floor for a second, and then back up to Briley. "How many men did Pemberton lose total?"

"Approximately 33,000 ... 3,000 casualties and almost 30,000 surrendered." His face furrowed as he spoke.

Eric frowned as he heard the news. "The Union has just effectively cut the South in half. They now control the Big Muddy from Minnesota to the Gulf ... I knew there was no way on God's green earth to fight a purely defensive battle without resupply of provisions or reinforcements."

Eric shook his head. "Sun Tzu taught us that. Thermopylae, Masada, the Alamo ... Shall I go on?"

The senior officer pointed at Schmidt. "See, gentleman, what a student of history can teach you? I told you this young Texan has a sound head on his shoulders."

General Briley reached into his desk and pulled out a manila envelope. It was addressed to Eric. "Have some orders that arrived by courier ealier today from your divison headquarters." He passed them to Eric's waiting hands.

He slipped his stag handled belt knife out of its scabbard and sliced the back flap open above the wax seal.

Returning the blade into its sheath without even looking, he pulled the first of three sheets of hand written pages from the light brown parcel.

Eric Schmidt, Lt. Col. CSA

To my most esteemed fellow officer. Word of your latest successful operation reached our headquarters and was shared with General Bobby Don Smith. He and I were quite pleased with the manner in which you have so ably accounted for yourself and your brave men deep in enemy held territory.

In recognition of your inspired leadership in repeated operational victories, he recommended a field promotion to the rank of full Colonel. I heartily concurred. At the present time, you will maintain command of the Second Regiment, Second Texas Cavalry. Nonetheless, I expect that you will be moved to a position as Brigade Commander when the proper opportunity presents itself.

I shall look forward to the opportunity to seeing you again here in Shreveport prior to your next assignment.

Sincerely yours,

Marcus Aurellius Matson, Major General, CSA Commander, First Division, Texas Cavalry

The young officer's mind raced. *I pray they let me stay with my own men. They are truly like the brothers I never had.*

General Briley watched the clouds come over the younger man's face. "Bad news, son?"

Eric shook his head. "I suppose I should be happy. My division commander notified me I was getting promoted again. The thought of eventually having to move up to brigade unfortunately gives me mixed feelings."

Briley nodded. "I understand ... But your men think quite highly of you. You earned that promotion."

"At least I am staying put for the meanwhile. Let me see what these other papers are." Eric removed two more pages. He read them, and then reread them a second time.

A furrow appeared in his youthful partially tanned forehead. It disappeared as his blue eyes sparkled for a moment. He chuckled. "I reckon all I need now is Moses and his walking stick."

The other officers glanced at each other with a slight case of bewilderment. General Briley spoke first. "How can that be of assistance?"

Eric grinned. "Gentlemen, correct me if I am ill informed, but the mighty Mississippi is crawling with Yankee gun boats ... especially in the area east of Shreveport around Vicksburg."

A senior colonel on Briley's staff nodded vigorously. "Thick as fleas and ticks on a coon dog, I hear."

"Exactly the way I envisioned it, I must say." The young colonel ran his fingers through his long blond hair. He held up the two page order. "The issue at hand, gentlemen, is my division commander and mentor, Major General Marcus Aurellius Matson, has ordered me to prepare an operational plan to escort two regiments of cavalry and mounted infantry reinforcements to join with the remnants of the Army of Mississippi."

He eyed General Briley. "They are to proceed eastward as soon as practicable to reinforce the men fighting in Alabama and Tennessee ... All I have to do now is devise a means to cross the Big Muddy without a Confederate Navy."

General Briley frowned as he crossed his arms and shook his head. "Not an easy task, I can assure you. That river is wide and the current is quite strong. It goes where it wants to go."

He pointed at one of his staff members. "Ask Colonel Andre Hebert here. He captained a side-wheeler up and down the river for over ten years before the war."

The forty year old dark haired lieutenant colonel grinned. "If had a silver dollar for every mile I wound my way up and down that crooked ol' waterway, I would own two or three plantations!"

Eric detected the strong French heritage the man came from immediately. "*Je suis sûr que tu aurais.*"

Andre's grin widened to a full smile. "Ah ... *Parlez vous Francais?*"

Eric grinned. "*Oui, mais seulement assez pour garder ma copine amusée.*"

His response brought a belly laugh from Lt. Colonel Hebert. "I would say you could keep your girlfriend amused very well. Your French is commendable ... Where does your lady friend live, if I might be so bold as to inquire?"

"Chateau LeBlanc, south of Shreveport."

"On the banks of the Red River," Andre responded. "I picked up a full load of cotton there on several occasions. My cousin George owns a bank in Shreveport. How are Augustin and his young daughter?"

"Quite well, according to her letters. I have not laid eyes on her in months," Eric said.

He shook his head. "What a small world."

General Briley smiled at the brief interaction. "Colonel Schmidt, I would think that Andre could answer many questions that you might have about the river and topography."

Eric nodded. "I would certainly appreciate that, sir. I do not plan to use one of the usual routes into Mississippi. My mind is already thinking of ways to get hundreds of men, horses, and wagons across."

"A logistical challenge, my friend, but not an impossibility." Andre began to dig into the stack of maps laid out on the desk.

He came up with one of eastern Arkansas, complete with rivers, towns, and plantations along the Mississippi. He turned to General Briley. "Sir, do you have a map of northern Mississippi handy?"

"Of course." He turned to the senior staff colonel. "Byron would you check the second drawer of the drafting table?"

The gray haired infantryman readily complied.

In a moment the two charts were laid side by side. Andre studied the two, and then pointed at the map. "See this little spot on the east bank? It is the remains of the Wilkinson Plantation in northern Mississippi. Perhaps forty miles south of Memphis … A Yankee gun boat landed there during the siege of Vicksburg. They burned it smooth to the ground."

Eric glanced at the map. "Looks as if they have decent roads going east from there. How far north of Vicksburg is that place?"

"Three hundred miles by river … one eighty-five as the crow flies."

Eric nodded slowly. "We need to talk."

§§§

CHAPTER NINE

SHREVEPORT, LOUISIANA

The town was bustling with traffic even before the train pulled into the station. Surreys, drays, Studebaker freight wagons, and numerous columns of cavalry jammed the streets, along with civilian mounted and foot traffic.

Bass Reeves watched a cloud of steam rumble and hiss along the passenger platform as the engineer released the pressure built up in the wood fired boiler. *My, oh, my. It already be hot and humid a'fore he went and did that.*

Some of the passengers got to their feet and began to collect their belongings at their feet and from the open overhead bins. The potbellied conductor entered the fifth and last passenger car and bellowed out his regular announcement, "Shreveport! ... Shreveport! End of the line, folks. Everybody off! Everybody off!" He turned around and headed back to the front of the train.

Bass grabbed hold of the bench seat in front of him, and pulled himself to his feet. He leaned left, and then right to try to straighten the kinks resulting from the unpadded birch seats.

He could see line after line of soldiers streaming out across the platform as they disembarked, and headed aft to claim their mounts from the eight livestock cars.

Bass peered into the bin and retrieved his hat. He pulled it on and got in line behind the white civilian passengers who were making for the left exit at the front of the car.

The big man took a couple of steps, stopped and rubbed his butt, trying to restore the circulation.

This ol' train done wore out its welcome comin' over from Marshall.

Outside on the platform, Bass looked around at his new surroundings. *My, My ... Would you look at all them people! They's all jammed together like at a fair or somethin'.*

He spotted his master walking with three other officers. The silver haired regiment commander, a lieutenant colonel, was giving instructions, "Get all the horses off safely, and see that the supply wagons get off loaded properly. Those muleskinners might need some help ... Line up and take a roll call."

Captain George Reeves nodded.

"Have your men walk your mounts into town. They have plenty of water troughs on the main street, as I recall. Water the animals, and then form up for a short ride to the bivouac area as we discussed."

He pointed at a bearded senior enlisted man walking up the ramp into the livestock car nearby. "The sergeant major will be in charge of setting up the tents. I, myself, will report to headquarters and check on further orders. Any questions?"

"No sir," the three company commanders replied in unison. They snapped a salute to the senior officer. He returned it, and headed toward the livestock cars.

Bass followed along behind the four soldiers in gray. He looked farther down the track, and saw one of the men from the regiment leading the dappled gray charger belonging to Lieutenant Colonel Armstrong down a heavily reinforced gangplank to the sun baked gravel alongside the railroad track. *Massa George called that there man the colonel's aide. Reckon that be a lot like me.*

The fresh faced lieutenant skillfully negotiated the three foot wide walkway without mishap. He handed the lead rope over to the colonel. "Here you are, sir. Have the cinch already tightened for you."

"Thank you, son," Colonel Armstrong replied. "Meet me at the headquarters building. You do remember the way, do you not?"

"Yes, sir. Of course."

The commander took hold of the reins and swung into the high backed McClellan saddle with a slight groan. His horse pranced around a bit. "Settle down, Trojan. You have not worked a lick all day."

The gelding came to a halt and whinnied once. Armstrong reined it north in the direction of Texas Street.

The regimental first sergeant had the bay mare onto the gravel before the colonel's horse made it into a fast walk. "Lieutenant, here she is … ready to ride."

The nineteen year old reached for the lead rope. "Ever so efficient, Sergeant. Duly noted." He crow hopped into the metal stirrup and swung aboard the bay. "See you men at the encampment."

He nudged the twelve year old into motion, and she responded like the well trained cavalry horse she was.

Bass watched the action and broke into a grin. *I sees now why they waited 'til last to board them horses. They ain't havin' to wait around like all the rest of us.*

George leaned closer to his counterpart in the Third Company. "I see the colonel's aide is right on top of things."

Major Art Shaeffer, a big man originally from Alexandria, Louisiana, spat a stream of dark tobacco juice onto the gravel.

He grinned broadly. "You ain't met the little whippersnapper yet, have you? He is the colonel's nephew ... wife's side of the family, of course. That's where he gets that red hair, and all them freckles. Smart enough, I suppose."

Art wiped the dribble of spittle off on the back side of his hand. "Hell, if he don't get hisself kilt the first time Yanks start to shootin' at us ..."

"You mean if he does not lose his water the first time, do you not?" Major Billy White, the First Company commanding officer chuckled as he cut in. "He might be a full colonel by Christmas." He laughed heartily.

Art broke into a broad grin.

Captain Reeves smiled somewhat sheepishly. "You boys have both seen some real action. How do you know that I will not cut and run when the bullets fly?"

Art looked at George incredulously. "You? Haw! You, sir, are made of sterner stuff. It was pretty damn rough around Grayson County back when you were sheriff."

Captain Reeves shrugged, and then nodded. "I 'spect you are right about that. But I never had to face cannon fire or a cavalry charge before … "

Billy slapped George on the back. "William Steel Reeves never raised a coward … Not from what I have seen. I do not think you have a thing to worry about."

He placed his hand on George's shoulder. "We will give you the benefit of our experience, and here is something else to chew on … Old man Armstrong saw service in the Mexican War. He even knows General Ulysses S. Grant, personally."

George's eyes grew wide. "Surely, you boys are pulling my leg!"

"Cross my heart and hope to die." Billy made an X across his chest.

Art nodded. "It is all true. Our regimental commander served with the Yankee general that just captured Vicksburg."

"Land o' Goshen," George muttered. "Cannot decide if that makes me feel better … or worse."

"Do not fret yourself, Captain. We have not even made it across the mighty Mississip, yet. That little feat might be a major undertaking all by itself."

"You know, Art, I had not given that a lot of thought ... what with everything coming together so quickly and all."

Billy smiled. "There is a saying in the military. *'That, my friend, is above my pay grade.'* Getting a whole cavalry regiment across a mile of enemy controlled river ... without the use of a navy, is logistical problem not left to some lowly company commander."

Bass walked up to the three officers. "Captain Reeves, you wants me to fetch both of our horses?"

"Surely do. Capital idea, Bass."

"Yassah." He headed to the wooden walkway and made his way up after a couple of other mounts were led down. Inside the livestock car, over a dozen horses were still tied up to the inside rail opposite the open doorway.

The wooden floor planks had been set a half inch apart to help drain the horse waste through, but it still was mighty slick and the smell would have driven a genteel person to tears. Bass spotted his mount tied up next to his master's.

"Howdy there, Whiskey. You made the trip just fine, I see. Gots to get the boss man's horse out first, but I will be back in a jiffy for you."

He patted the horse's neck and untied Dollar's lead rope. "Easy, big boy, easy now. We will walk out nice and slow. No monkey business, you hear? Do not act a fool, and we gonna be out of here a'for you knows it."

He stroked the big gray's neck and rubbed his calloused hand across the pony's nose. "Come on, let us get outta this stinkin' hot box. What do you say?"

Carefully, he led the way to the gangplank and then shortened his grip in the lead rope. "Jest take it slow, boy. Everything gonna be just fine," he whispered in Dollar's ear. Arriving down on the firm ground once more, he loosened his grip and slid down lower on the lead rope and stepped farther in front of the horse.

"Massa Reeves, figured you wanted to set you own cinch just like you want it. Is that right?"

"Until I tell you different, that is correct. A man gets mighty particular about his rigging."

"He do." Bass turned back to the livestock car.

Twenty minutes later, the bulk of the cavalry mounts were off loaded.

On the flatbed cars, groups of cavalrymen were helping the teamsters turn the long wagon tongues almost ninety degrees to the side.

Other teamsters were rigging up pairs of horses to their traces and lining them up on the earthen ramps adjacent to the narrow freight docks. Several soldiers helped back the teams up into place where the wagon tongues lay between the two horses.

With years of experience the wagoneers quickly hitched the teams to the heavy hewn oaken timbers. The drivers would carefully unroll the leather ribbon and toss them up and across the empty seats.

A young corporal from Tyler climbed aboard the first wagon to made ready. He spat a stream of tobacco down between his feet as his lifted the reins.

He pointed at some troops standing on the thirty degree slope. "You boys best get clear. Once I get this load started down that there … ain't nuthin' short of God hisself gonna be able to stop it."

The men heeded his warning. He took the slack out of the reins and wrapped them around three fingers of his gloved hands. Pulling slight tension on the left lead, he gently popped both on the rumps of the team. "Haw up there, you hay burners. Time's a wastin'."

With a mournful creak of leather and a high pitched squeak from a wooden wheel on its axle, the team leaned into their traces and began to move the green Studebaker from atop the flatbed rail car.

Moving slowly at first, the front wheels crossed over the steel strips laid down to fill the gap between the rail car and the dock. Once they crested the flat planks of the six foot wide dock, they picked up momentum and speed.

The muleskinner straightened the ribbons and pushed forward on the foot brake as he reined back on the team. The pair of horses struggled to get the heavy load arrested but brought it to a full stop only sixty feet past the end of the ramp.

His assistant climbed aboard, and they drove the wagon two hundred yards onto Texas street and parked it. "Well, sir, we look to be first in line in this fandango." The corporal looked over his shoulder as the same scene was repeated two dozen times. He turned and studied the layout of Shreveport. "Wish I had me a dime ... I would be sendin' you over to that saloon to bring us both a beer."

"I would be might proud to fetch it, too. Some kind of hot out here in the sun."

§§§

CHAPTER TEN

SHREVEPORT OUTSKIRTS

The two Confederate officers continued the road trot pace that they had begun since leaving Texarkana. They had only stopped briefly to water the horses and stretch their own legs.

Colonel Eric Schmidt noticed the new construction going up on both sides of the road. "My, oh, my. Can hardly believe the changes in the last three months. Shreveport's busting out at the seams."

His companion, Colonel Andre Hebert agreed, "Although this is my first time to travel this particular stretch of road, I must agree that the area appears to be prospering ... Wonder if the river front has changed as much in the time since I left my position on that side-wheeler?"

"I suppose we shall find out when we get to town."

The traffic along Texarkana Road thickened as the pair got closer to Texas Street. They slowed to a trot as they weaved and wound their way between slower moving wagons moving in both directions.

Hundreds of cavalry men were spread out up and down Texas Street, the town's main east-west road. Their unit colors were displayed on new wooden guidons carried at the front of each company.

A stiff southwest breeze had begun to blow and caused the small flags to unfurl as the brigade was called to attention.

Eric reined to a halt. He pointed toward the lead company in the column. "I bet that's the unit we are directed to get across the Big Muddy ... See the

Texas flag? Must belong to the new 11th and 12th regiments of volunteers from back home."

Andre nodded. "There certainly are good number of them." He studied the wagons at the rear of the formation. "We shall have a bit of a challenge getting them all across ... There is quiet a lot of tonnage involved."

A bugler at the head of the column of cavalry and mounted infantry sounded assembly. The unit executive officer shouted out, "Eleventh Regiment ... report!"

The company commanders barked out their replies in sequence.

Satisfied with the "All men present or accounted for" reports, the major led the assembled units out in columns of three at a walk.

A few hundred yards to the east, a distinguished balding man escorted a young woman with flowing scarlet tresses out to a barouche open top carriage tied up outside the bank.

A middle aged black man dressed with a starched white cotton shirt and black slacks sat atop the leather covered driver's seat of the shiny emerald green carriage. He quickly stepped down as the couple approached and opened the half door on the side closest to the boardwalk.

"Afternoon, Mister Hebert. I trust today's tutoring session went well."

Charles nodded and grinned. "It certainly did. Miss LeBlanc is quiet the apt pupil."

Angelina blushed slightly as she grabbed a hand hold on the carriage and stepped up the gracefully curved running board on the side and then up onto the floor of the conveyance. "You flatter me, Mister Hebert. I have so much to learn … There is significantly more than just holding customer deposits in safekeeping."

The banker grinned. "And you shall learn it all in due time. It is a joy teaching you." Charles dipped his head once. "See you in two days."

Angelina took her seat on the tufted burgundy colored leather bench. She looked up at the scorching summer sun. Even in her lightest weight off-white silk charmeuse dress, the heat was considerable.

Cyrus caught the slight frown that crossed her face as he closed the door and latched it. "Would you like the sun top put up, Miss Angelina?"

"If you do not mind too terribly, Cyrus. I hate to be a bother."

He smiled. "You can never be a bother to me. It is my job to keep you safe, sound, and as comfortable as I can."

He stepped up on the running board and grasped the frame of the folding convertible top. With one swift move, he tugged the canvas cover from its stowed position aft of the passenger seat.

He snapped down the hinged locking mechanism to keep the top taut and the sun off his passenger.

"There you are, young lady. This should make the ride much more pleasant ... I remember your mama used to like being out of the afternoon sun this time of year, just like you."

He smiled at the memory of Elouise LeBlanc. Angelina's mother had died giving birth to her, and her daughter had grown up to bear an uncanny resemblance to the mother she never knew.

Cyrus hopped down, closing the half door behind him. He untied the team's lead rope and secured it on the sleek jet black Standardbred on the left.

Climbing back to the driver's seat, he grabbed the reins and deftly coaxed the matched pair into motion.

Bass Reeves was happy when the procession in front of him had finally made enough progress and the wagons he followed began to roll.

Lawdy, Lawdy ... It gonna take us a month of Sundays to go fifteen hundred miles at this rate. "Come on, Whiskey. Do not you let us get lost, boy. All we gots to do is follow them wagons to the camp."

He squeezed his knees on the sorrel Morgan's ribcage. The big gelding fell in line without even a hint of a protest.

Bass spotted two mounted Confederate officers watching the convoy from a vantage point at the intersection of the Texarkana road and Texas Street.

The blonde haired lieutenant colonel smiled at him and touched the brim of his hat when Bass tipped his hat at the pair of officers.

That seems like a nice fella. Kinda young though. He don't look to be as old as I am. He watched as the two turned and walked their horses eastbound on the same street as the regiment.

"Where in Texas are you men from?" asked the younger of the pair of officers.

"Well, sah, we be from up Grayson county way. A bit northwest of Sherman, if'n you knows where that be."

"I do … Come from just east of Tyler, myself. Welcome to Shreveport."

"Yassah. Thank you, sah." Bass grinned. *I reckon they be a lot more Texans over here than I knowed about.*

The lead units of the column turned right onto River Street, a major thoroughfare that ran roughly parallel to the Red River. Many of the local residents lined the boardwalks watching the procession as if it were a parade.

Cyrus reined the carriage to a halt when he spotted how congested the route had become. "Sorry, Miss Angelina. Looks like it will be a few minutes before this clears."

"I see. There must be hundreds of them … They most likely have just arrived on the train from Marshall."

The sight of the Texas flags reminded her of Eric. She opened her handbag and pulled out one of his letters. Although she had already read it through four times, a fifth would do no harm.

Colonel Schmidt spotted a familiar face perched up on the seat of a fancy barouche near the intersection with River Street. His eyes immediately went to the passenger seated in the rear.

Although she was mostly shaded by the canvas top, her delicate features and flowing red hair brought a huge smile to his face.

"Andre, my friend, I think luck is with us today." Eric reined to a halt.

Andre pulled up and shot a quick glance over to his traveling companion. "If you say so, Colonel. In what respect would you characterize our good fortune?"

Eric continued to smile broadly. "Do you remember Cyrus from the Chateau LeBlanc?"

"Of course ... Good man, he is."

"If my eyes do not deceive me, he is driving that fine carriage about seventy five yards up ahead." He pointed with his gloved hand held low between himself and his traveling companion.

"Ah," Andre responded. "What good eyes you have. Is that your young lady friend in the back? ... Forgive me. What a foolish question." He chuckled.

"Why else would he be grinning like a possum eating persimmons?"

"It would appear that Cyrus is waiting for the traffic to subside before making the turn toward home. Give me a few seconds to set up my surprise ... Drop by and pay your respects, if you like."

"As you wish." Andre watched as Eric reined left, skirting the boardwalk while keeping his head tilted down—The brim of his cavalry hat covered his face to those people looking westward.

Once Eric was almost in position, Lt. Colonel Hebert nudged his mount into motion. He closed the distance to the carriage as Eric passed behind it and came to a halt behind the parked carriage.

"Cyrus, wonderful to see you, my good man." He held up his right hand as he waved.

The affable black driver grinned. "Captain Hebert! I did not know you had joined the army. You, sir, are a sight for sore eyes."

Angelina's concentration in her reading was broken by the conversation. She looked up and smiled. "So that's where you have been ... Father and I wondered why you were no longer plying the waters of the Red ... My, do you not look dashing in uniform, Colonel."

"I leave you for a few months and suddenly, everybody in uniform is dashing?"

Angelina spun around at the sound of a dearly missed voice. A tall, tanned blond officer was standing beside the coach with his arms crossed on top of the passenger door. "Eric! Why did you not tell me ?"

She lunged to the left side of the carriage, placed both hands on his upturned face and planted a passionate kiss on his lips.

He returned the passion and held her close. "Oh how I missed you."

Tears of joy streamed down her cheeks. "I've been praying for your safe return every single day … father has been, too."

"We appreciate that … we all do. Isn't that right, Andre?"

The dark haired colonel agreed, "Prayers always are a blessing for us. Those and letters from home."

Angelina wiped the tears from her eyes with her finger tip. She held up the letter from Eric. "Fifth time for this one. I just received it a few days ago."

"Did not want to let you think I forgot you. That will never happen."

She kissed him again. "How long will you be here this time?"

He shook his head. "Cannot say ... I do plan to stay the night. Do you and your father have room for a pair of uninvited guests?" He grinned.

She playfully slapped him lightly on the left shoulder, sending up a tiny cloud of reddish road dust from his tunic. "Silly you. Of course we do, my love. You and Andre are always welcome ... I see that you could use a bit of freshening up after your journey."

Angelina brushed the Louisiana clay off her hands in a bit of theatrics.

Eric laughed. "Yes, Ma'am. The thought of a hot bath and sleeping in a real bed is just short of heaven. Is that not so, Andre?"

"As for myself, I am looking forward to it."

"Then, it is settled. We will hold dinner until you arrive. No doubt you must first check in with your generals or some such thing."

"Quite perceptive of you, my dear." Eric nodded. "Have some business at the headquarters, but we shall see you and your father this evening."

§§§

CHAPTER ELEVEN

TRANS-MISSISSIPPI DEPARTMENT
CONFEDERATE ARMY HEADQUARTERS
SHREVEPORT, LOUISIANA

With the fall of Vicksburg, the role of Shreveport in the War Between the States became paramount. The loss of free access to the mouths of the Mississippi River in New Orleans and subsequently the Red

River led to the establishment of the primary western headquarters of the Confederacy in the bustling river port town only a scant few road miles from the eastern Texas border.

The two road-weary cavalry officers reined in front of the two story wooden frame building and found one of a few open spots available at the hitching posts lining the cypress plank boardwalk.

Eric dismounted first, tossed the metal stirrup over the McClellen saddle seat, and loosened the cinch on his black stallion. He tied his lead rope off, giving Lightning enough slack to reach the water trough.

Lt. Colonel Hebert followed suit but rubbed his backside to restore the circulation after the long ride. "Never realized what an easy life I lived on the river. Everything I needed was right there on board."

He glanced over at Eric as he retrieved his highly sensitive travel orders from his saddle bags. The younger officer was still beaming. "Well, almost everything."

Eric slapped his dusty cavalry hat against his thigh, and then snugged it back down on his head.

He removed his riding gloves, and slipped them under his uniform belt, neatly folding the sweat-stained leather to keep them from sliding loose.

Andre untied a leather map case from behind his soogan. The men made their way into the headquarters past the two outside sentries. Eric spotted a familiar face, a young officer from Texarkana. "Captain Applewhite, how are you these days?"

The sandy haired twenty four year old got to his feet and saluted him. "Doing fine, Colonel. General Matson is looking forward to seeing you, sir."

"As am I ... May I introduce Lieutenant Colonel Andre Hebert?" He turned to his compatriot. "Andre, Captain Arthur Applewhite is aide to General Matson."

Colonel Hebert extended his hand and greeted the younger man. "My pleasure, sir."

"The pleasure is mine, Colonel. I believe I know your cousin Charles ... He is one of Shreveport's leading citizens and a prominent banker in these parts."

Eric grinned. "The grass does not grow under the captain's feet. Very little gets past his eye."

Andre chuckled. "See what you mean. That must be why the General chose him."

The captain shook his head. "You gentlemen are far too kind. But, speaking of my boss, he is up in his office going over some plans with the Sixth and Eighth Regiment commanders. Permit to escort you … please follow me."

Captain Applewhite knocked twice on the closed wooden door, and then opened it for the senior officers, and then followed them inside.

Major General Marcus Aurellius Matson looked up from a map table. A smile came to his face when he saw his protégé enter. "Finally … Gents, here is the man I have tasked with the logistics of the river crossing."

Eric and Andre saluted the senior officer, and he returned a salute before extending his hand.

"Outstanding mission up north, Eric. Really proud of you."

Colonel Schmidt shook Matson's hand. "Thank you sir, but I did not do it single handedly. I owe the mission's success to my men. They performed admirably … May I introduce Colonel Andre Hebert? He has many years experience on the

Mississippi and Red Rivers as a steamboat captain. I found his insights most valuable."

"How fortunate." The general shook the lieutenant colonel Hcberts's hand as well. "Pleased to have you aboard, Colonel."

"Thank you, sir. Colonel Schmidt speaks very highly of you. I am here to assist this mission in any way possible."

Matson nodded his head. "I am doubly certain that I picked the right man for the job now. See you staffed your weakness, Eric."

He grinned. "Only following your lead, sir … You taught me that I did not have to be the smartest one, but to surround myself with those who are."

Matson laughed. He turned to Captain Applewhite. "Arthur can you rustle up some brandy or cream sherry and six glasses? Surely these gentlemen have some trail dust that needs to be washed down … Let me introduce our newcomers to the men commanding the forces they are going to transport across the Big Muddy."

"As you wish, sir." The aide departed the room and quietly closed the door behind him.

Buck Stienke

PASTURE SOUTH OF SHREVEPORT

Bass was pleasantly surprised when the procession of wagons and mounted soldiers arrived in a sprawling pasture south of town. The eastern edge was lined with towering cypress trees along the Red River while the western boundary was a forest of century-old live oaks festooned with long beards of gray Spanish moss hanging low.

He noted a series of small poles sticking out of the ground—many had small hand lettered signs, while others had colored cloth differentiating the cavalry from mounted infantry. As he got closer, he could see various unit designations on them.

Different units peeled off from the column and followed arrows to their individual bivouac areas.

Ain't that somethin? Always wondered how they got them tents all lined up neat and orderly like. How in blazes am I gonna find out where Captain Reeves and I belong?

Bass followed a freight wagon as it made its turn to the Third Company area and came to a stop. Several men began to surround the tailgate as the

146

muleskinner set the brake and climbed down from the bench seat.

He watched as they lowered the tailgate and began pulling off some heavy tan tents for the mess facility. One of the junior enlisted men turned to Bass, who still was astride his horse.

"Hey, boy, why doncha get down and give us a hand here? That is if you want to eat tonight."

"Yassah." He ground tied the sorrel and patted its neck. "Mind you can graze a bit whilst I help these mens get this tent thing all put up."

He looked around to see if he could spot his master. Captain Reeves and his gray horse were not visible in the throng of people going about the task of making camp.

Well, at least I did not get myself lost. Reckon one of these Johnnie Rebs knows where we are s'pposed to be stayin'.

Twenty minutes later, the mess tents were erected and the camp cooks had a dozen fire pits dug, the iron tripods in place.

Large cast iron pots were suspended over the wood fires, heating up dabs of lard before the vegetables were cooked. Other men on the mess detail were plucking freshly killed chickens for the soup.

Still others were mixing corn meal, salt, pepper, and water with a dash of baking soda. Dozens of large Dutch ovens—flat bottomed cast iron pots with depressed lids, designed to hold coals—were being made ready.

Cooks greased the inside with once-white cotton kitchen towels dipped into large tins of lard.

Bass wiped the sweat from his brow on the back of his riding gloves. The temperature was still in the low 90s, and the Louisiana humidity was even higher than that of his home town. He looked around and still could not see his master.

The big man walked up to a corporal that he had helped raise one of the main tent poles. "'Scuse me there, sir. Y'all know where I can find Captain George Reeves?"

The soldier glanced back at him. "What company is he with?"

Bass shook his head. "Don't rightly know … All I know is that he be with the calvary."

His response brought a smile. "Calvary is where they crucified Jesus … Mounted soldiers who fight from horseback are called *cavalry*."

"Cav … cavalry. I will get that right from now on. 'Preciate it." Bass nodded. "But do you know where he might be?"

"The Eleventh is south of here." He pointed toward that direction. "That is where the cavalry is. The Twelfth division is mounted infantry, and they are behind us, back toward town."

"Much obliged," Bass said with a huge grin.

"Any time." The corporal stuck out his hand. "Thanks for the help. Those poles on these big tents are way too much for one man."

Bass shook his hand firmly. "You be welcome … A little hard work never scared me a'tall."

The corporal grinned. "Do not imagine it would." *Hate to have that big son of a gun mad at me. He could squash me like a bug with those big fists.*

Bass grabbed the reins to Whiskey and swung into the saddle. "Come on, you hay burner. We needs to find our massa a'fore it gets dark."

TRANS-MISSISSIPPI DEPARTMENT CONFEDERATE ARMY HEADQUARTERS SHREVEPORT, LOUISIANA

Colonels Schmidt and Hebert finished laying out his daring plan. The two division commanders exchanged nervous glances. Their looks did not go unnoticed by the Major General.

"Gentlemen, I imagine that you have some questions for the operational commander ...That is, unless you think we should move on Vicksburg and fight our way across the river."

Both of them shook their heads.

General Matson turned to Eric. "For a short notice operational plan, I must say I am impressed. That being said, what additional supplies will you need to make your ferry a reality?"

Eric's face took on a serious countenance. "A small portable steam powered sawmill, carpentry tools, nails, pitch, and, of course, sufficient rope and cable to span the river ... steel hubs for the cable pulleys."

He took in a deep breath. " A handful of skilled boat builders would be a plus. And a blacksmith … or two."

Matson nodded. "I believe we can find those skills among the men of the division … Not certain about boat builders, but I know there are men here in Shreveport who live on the water. We can check about a saw mill."

"Augustin LeBlanc has one on his plantation. I will inquire over dinner tonight."

"Capital idea. Have you been in touch with that young lady who resides in the Chateau LeBlanc?"

Eric once more broke into a huge grin. "As a matter of fact, Colonel Hebert and I ran into her and her driver Cyrus just this afternoon on the way here."

"You do lead a charmed life my friend." General Matson held up his right index finger. "I almost forgot." He stepped over to his pecan wood desk and opened the top right hand drawer.

He pulled out a small black cardboard box, approximately three inches wide by five inches tall and one inch thick. Marcus handed it to Eric.

"In normal circumstances, we would have a ceremony and reception for this august event. In light of present exigencies of the service, I shall forgo that pomp and circumstance. Congratulations on your promotion, Colonel."

Eric opened the lid of the box to find two silver wire embroidered stars lying in a blue velvet liner. He picked one up and felt the weight of the insignia. "Thank you, General Matson. I will do my best to honor your faith in my abilities."

"I know that you will." He glanced over at the bottle of brandy. "Gentlemen, I propose a toast to the South's newest Colonel and to the success of your mission."

§§§

CHAPTER TWELVE

CHATEAU LEBLANC

Angelina walked to the pair of French doors overlooking the portico with the view of the sun setting in the west. She peered through the leaded glass panes of a pair of ornate French doors leading to the covered porch. Seeing nothing, save the cotton fields that extended all the way to the horizon, she let out an audible sigh.

Augustin LeBlanc laid his hand on her shoulder. "What is that old saying about a watched pot?"

She spun around and blushed slightly. "Am I that obvious, Father?"

"Of course you are, my dear. I have watched you every day for the past twenty years ... Would you grant me the common sense to know your every mood?"

He caught sight of some movement in the right side of the field of view though the portal. Two Confederate officers were making their way down the sidewalk toward the steps. One of the plantation's young household staff members carried their saddlebags.

Augustin nodded in their direction and smiled. "Company approaches."

Angelina's green eyes flew open wide as she gasped slightly and wheeled around. Her lilac hoop skirted dress was slightly slower in rotation than her upper body. The floor length garment finally caught up with her and continued past her 180 degree turn and eventually settled into position. She reached for the curved brass handle to the left door and turned it downward.

Colonel Eric Schmidt grinned broadly at the sight of his beloved red head charging out onto the bricked patio. He held out his arms to give her a hug. "You look lovely in that color."

She jumped into his arms and wrapped her arms around him. "I have been counting every minute until you arrive."

The master of the expansive estate laughed. "I can attest to that fact ... For the life of me, I cannot recall the last time she was so anxious."

Eric lowered the petite woman to the ground and extended a hand. "A pleasure to see you again, sir."

Augustin took his hand and shook it firmly. "We both have missed you, young man. We pray for your safekeeping every day."

Leblanc glanced to the other officer. "I see you brought a friend of ours with you." He released his grip with Eric and reached for the former steamboat captain. "Welcome back to Chateau Leblanc, Captain ... or should I say Colonel Hebert?"

Andre grinned broadly as he shook the hand of the wealthy planter. "Augustin, my friend, it is indeed a pleasure to see you once again. Just call me Andre, if you prefer." He looked around the property. "You know, this is my first time visiting here on horseback. Looks quite different than from the riverboat's vantage point."

"Let us go back inside, gentlemen. It is much cooler inside than out."

"That is a marvelous suggestion, Father." Angelina turned to the young black man holding two pairs of saddlebags. "Marvin, please deposit their things in the guest suites. Have two baths drawn … I am certain they will want to freshen up before dinner."

"Yes, Ma'am." He broke away from the group as they entered the great room.

She glanced back to Eric and gave him an almost imperceptible wink.

He turned to his host. "Mister LeBlanc, we hate to inconvenience you so much. Surely you regularly dine much earlier that this."

Augustin shook his head. "Think nothing of it, young man. I was delighted that you are safe and accepted my daughter's invitation to stay with us … Besides, we do not entertain much this time of year. I, for one, am looking forward to having conversations with friends who are up on current events."

Andre nodded his agreement. "As a matter of fact, I have been posted up in Arkansas for the last few months. It will be enlightening hearing how you are planning to deal with the loss of the Mississippi export channel."

A serious look came across the planter's face. "It will be a challenge this fall, indeed. Perhaps you two can inform me on the status of the Texas ports and the Union blockade."

The five stopped near the base of the gracefully curved staircase to the upper floors. Cyrus appeared, as if on cue, carrying a silver platter with the appropriate number of small crystal glasses filled with a dark liquid.

"Would you gentlemen care for a bit of aged sherry to cleanse the palate after your long day in the saddle?"

Eric and Andre exchanged glances. The blonde haired colonel looked to Angelina. "Only if you join us."

"But, of course," she said with a slight courtesy.

Cyrus offered her a glass first, and then served Augustin and their guests.

The elder LeBlanc held up the cut crystal and proposed a toast. "To good friends, peace and prosperity."

They all sipped the warm aromatic libation ... savoring the complex flavors as the aroma of the sherry wafted up.

Andre smiled. "A hint of cherries, with a touch of tobacco and an oak finish. Excellent vintage, Monsieur LeBlanc."

"From our own vines, brought here from Saint-Emillion."

"I am not familiar with that name," Eric observed.

"A small town in southwest France ... I believe it is near Bordeaux, is that not true, Father?"

Augustin nodded his agreement. "Your geography is exemplary, young lady."

"I have heard of Bordeaux, of course," Eric added. "It is famous for the wine of the same name."

Andre nodded. "Yes, but technically, Bordeaux is a blend of Cabernet Sauvignon and Merlot." He shrugged.

Eric chuckled. "I love the way you three talk. For some reason, foreign wines spoken with a

French accent sound so much better than when we Texans say it."

The others laughed.

Angelina pointed upstairs. "The faster you two can get bathed and changed, the faster we can begin dinner. Please leave your boots outside in the hallway, and one of the servants will blacken them while you get ready."

Eric smiled. "Yes, Ma'am. We shall not keep you waiting long." He turned to climb the oaken stairwell, but suddenly, a thought came to him. "By any chance do you have a seamstress on staff?"

"Of course, what do you need mended?"

"Not exactly mended … " he fished inside his tunic and drew out something in his hand. "I have been promoted to full colonel and need one of these stars sewn to the collar on each side."

He held up one of the silver badges, and then handed it to her.

Her face broke into a huge smile. "Oh Eric, I am so proud of you!" She turned to Augustin. "Father, is that not great news?"

'Congratulations, Colonel. You must be making a huge impression with someone."

"The credit goes to my men, sir … I merely tell them what we need to do and then lead the way."

Angelina shook her head. "Leave your dusty uniforms out in the hall as well. Assume you brought a change of clothes."

The two officers nodded their affirmation.

"Excellent. I shall have Sarah clean and press them for you, and if she cannot affix the little stars, I can handle a needle and thread myself."

"That would be wonderful," Eric said as he gave her one last, longing look before he turned to ascend the stairs.

Eric combed his still-damp golden hair straight back and felt a few drops of water fall on the shoulders of his clean union suit.

Gonna have to get a haircut soon or this shaggy mess will start to make me look like a Neanderthal.

The full length guest room mirror was trimmed in gold leaf and culminated in an ornate hand carved sea shell. He stared for a moment at his refection — the man did not bear much rescmblance to the clean shaven apprentice gunsmith that he had been the previous year.

The faces of his men, the battles he had seen and places that had become part of his new life in the Confederate cavalry seemed almost like a dream.

Eric pulled on the tan canvas pants he had specially placed in his saddlebags for the trip to Shreveport. He unwrapped the brown butcher paper covering the crisply starched white cotton shirt.

He donned it as quickly as he could get the buttons fastened, flipped up the collar, and then tied the simple black cravat into a bow as he looked into the mirror. Eric turned the collar down and insured his tie was centered.

His image reminded him of the first time he met the beautiful Angelina. That upscale restaurant, called Antoine's, was where the Shreveport CSA detachment commander, a Major Joseph Robinson, took it upon himself to introduce the hero of the day to the local elite of northern Louisiana society.

Eric laughed. *And here it is, more than a year later, and I am still wearing one of the only two sets of civilian clothes to my name.*

He opened the door to the hallway, and found his knee-high riding boots cleaned and polished. *These have not looked this good since the day I bought them.* He took a seat on a small fabric covered bench in the hall and tugged them on over his wool socks.

Looking down the hall, he saw that there were still two cavalry boots outside the adjoining room. He tapped on the door lightly. "How much longer, Andre?"

The dark haired lieutenant colonel opened the door as he tucked his shirttail into the back of his pants.

"I will not keep you waiting. I know who is waiting impatiently downstairs."

Eric handed the boots to Andre. "Here is a handy place to pull those on." He pointed at the settee.

Hebert grinned and took a seat. "First class operation all around." He looked at Eric. "How long since you were out of that uniform?"

The young colonel shook his head. "Fourteen months? Something like that ... It feels ... "

"Different? Tonight will be like a holiday of sorts." His face took on a more somber countenance. "Enjoy your time with Angelina tonight, my friend. We are not promised tomorrow."

§§§

CHAPTER THIRTEEN

CONFEDERATE CAMP

Bass wiped the sweat from his brow with the red handkerchief and shoved it deep in the rear pocket of his overalls. He took in a deep breath and slowly let it out.

Looking at the row upon row of tents that had been pitched on the pasture south of Shreveport, he shook his head. *We gots to do this every time we move from place to place? Lordy , Lordy ... These army folks ain't never gonna get much fightin' done. They be a spendin' all they time jus gettin' ready to sleep and eat.*

With his saddlebags slung over his shoulders, he made his way back to the area he was told that Captain Reeves would be bivouacked. He spotted his master talking with another company commander. Bass approached George but held up a few feet away and did not announce his presence.

After a minute or so, Major Shaeffer spotted him and tilted his head in the slave's direction. "Appears he did not get lost after all."

Captain George Reeves turned to Bass. His brown eyes narrowed. "Where in blue blazes have you been, boy? I have been looking for you for almost two hours."

Bass pointed back to the north. "Well, Massa, me and some of them army mens has been a puttin' them cook tents ... and that big un where everybody eats."

The scowl never left the major's face. "You mean the mess tent?"

Bass shook his head. "Nawsah, it be all neat and orderly when we wuz done through with it."

Major Shaeffer stifled a laugh.

George shook his head. "It's called a mess tent. That the army word for a dining facility."

Bass nodded. "Yassah. I tries to 'member that from now on."

"It took two hours to just erect the two tents?" The captain was clearly not happy.

"Nawsah. After we done got them tent things all stood up, and drove them little stakes in the ground, and tied off the ropes, one of them army mens asked me to help him rig up a picket line for the horses. Kinda reminds me of a clothes line but not as tall … since they ain't no trees 'cepting way over yonder…"

Bass pointed to the western edge of the pasture. "… we had to dig some holes and set poles in the ground. Then I started a lookin' for you, but most folks, they did not know who you was."

Art shook his head. "They have the unit markings on the little signs where we turned off the main trail." He thumbed back toward the east.

"Yassah. Reckon they do." Bass nodded his agreement. " But the thing is, I don't know what the name of Massa George's outfit is … And 'sides that, I cain't read a lick." He shrugged his broad shoulders.

Captain Reeves glanced over at Art. "See what I have to deal with?" He then eyed Bass. "I should not have to point out that an officer does not erect his own tent ... have been waiting far, far too long for your arrival. For your future information, my current station is as the commander of the Second Company, Eleventh Cavalry. Do not forget that."

Bass bobbed his head quickly. "Yassah ... uh, I mean, nawsah. I won't be forgettin' ... Second Company. I be rememberin' that."

The officers walked a few yards to the spot where a light tan colored canvas tent was rolled up neatly. Beside it were a painted wooden trunk, a folded up cot, and a bed roll. The captain's Texas Hope saddle was left atop the trunk, the wooden stirrups crossed neatly over the seat.

An eight foot tall center pole, complete with a with a small metal rod protruding from one end, and a handful of foot long wooden stakes—each sharpened to a sixty degree point—lay waiting.

"Now get your butt over here and get my tent set up. It's almost time for dinner."

Bass did so without comment. The two officers sauntered off toward the distant mess tent. Bass looked at the tent stakes. *Ain't got me no hammer to drive them things in this sun baked black gumbo.* He glanced around at all the other smaller tents already set up. *Somebody has to have one or, at least, a big ol' mallet.*

He walked up to a pair of young privates. Neither of the lads came up to his shoulder. He did not know the names of either one. "'Scuse, me gentlemens. Is y'all in the Second Company?"

The sandy hair sixteen year old turned to him. "You know it. What can we do you for?"

Bass grinned. "I be needin' me a sludge hammer or maybe one of them big ol' mallets with steel rings 'round it to set up Captain Reeves tent. Y'all know where a man can find one?"

The other private, a seventeen year old from Corsicana with straggly brown hair down to his shoulders, chuckled. "We ain't got one, but our sergeant do, fo' shore. He keeps purty close tabs on it."

"Can you tell me who that would be? All you soldier boys kinda look alike to me."

Both privates laughed out loud. The sandy haired one with pimples spoke up, "Happens to us, too. We only volunteered two weeks ago."

"Come on … Sergeant Simmons will get you fixed right up … He's from Corsicana, too. I know both his little brothers."

The three went a hundred yards down the row of tents and came up to a red-haired man in his early twenties. "Hey, Red. This here colored man needs to borry yore sledge hammer to set up the captain's tent."

"Do he now?" He looked Bass over with a jaundiced eye. "What's your name, boy?"

"Folks call me Bass Reeves." He smiled broadly.

"And you are setting up a tent for our Captain Reeves? He any kin to you?"

Bass let go a deep belly laugh and shook his head. "Not 'xactly … See, his pappy owned my pappy, and now he owns me."

The three white soldiers exchanged nervous glances. Red went to his tent and pulled out an eight pound sledge hammer with a stout hickory handle. He held it out for Bass. "Here you go. Now, you bring it back in one piece … it's the onlyest one I got."

Bass took hold of it and flipped it end over end, snatching the grip of the handle like a cobra striking. "A little lighter than the one I uses back on the farm, but it will do jest fine. Much obliged, Sergeant Red."

The much smaller non commissioned officer smiled. "You two go help Mister Reeves get the captain's tent put up. Make sure I get my hammer back. Understand?"

"Yes, Sergeant," the two younger cavalrymen replied as one.

Bass tipped his hat at the NCO before he turned away. *I will have to remember that one. He called me Mister Reeves.*

Bass tugged the last of the eight sisal tent ropes tight to their stakes. *That ought to hold agin the wind, if'n we get any.*

The young soldiers offered to return the coveted hammer. "Thank you kindly, gents. It was a mite easier getting this thing up with three of us. I 'preciate it." He handed them the heavy tool.

"Ain't no thang, Bass ... Sides, Red told us to help you," Richard said with a slight shrug.

"I understands, but I wants y'all to know much it means to me." He looked both ways down the row of tents. "Ain't got much to my name, but I reckon you mens might like a little treat for y'all's efforts."

He slipped inside the tent and pulled a small paper sack from his saddlebags. "You boys like penny candy?"

The teenagers looked at one another with astonishment clearly written of their faces. The younger one spoke up first. "Are you kiddin? Everybody likes candy."

Bass grinned. "Gots me some peppermint sticks, hoarshounds, Turkish delights and Neccos ... Sorry, but I done ate up all them Jordan almonds." He held open the sack. "Get yourself one."

Richard took out a peppermint stick. "My mama used to buy these in Corsicana, come Christmas time."

"Go ahead, Michael. You get to pick one, too. Bought these just yesterday in Sherman."

"Thank you, Bass. Believe I will." He stared in the sack for a moment and then reached in and grabbed a Turkish delight. "Love these little boogers. They are sweet and hot at the same time."

"Got that right." Bass' eyes crinkled. "Enjoy it."

Richard rolled the peppermint stick around in his mouth like it was a cigar. He stuck out his hand. "Thanks for rememberin' me what it was like."

Bass shook his hand firmly, and smiled broadly.

Michael shook the big man's hand as well. "Anytime you need some more muscle, call on us."

Bass chuckled as he looked over the two skinny teenagers. "I surely will."

Two hundred yards to the north, a potbellied cook approached a steel triangle hung from the center ridge pole of the mess tent. He carried a three foot long fire poker used to keep the firewood coals pushed under the huge cooking pots.

With something of a flourish, he took both hands and rattled the blackened poker around the insides of the triangle. The bell-like ringing could be heard a half mile around.

"Soup's on! Come and get it 'til it's gone!" he bellowed and turned to move to the head of one of the four serving lines.

"Chow time," Richard said with his East Texas twang. "Grab your bowl or plate. "We will get ol' hammer back to Red an' see ya up yonder."

"Sounds good to me … Been a bit since we last eat," Bass said.

By the time Bass got up to the mess area, many of the officers were seated on benches set alongside the half dozen tables under the large tent. The lines of enlisted men were over seventy-five soldiers long and less than half the two regiments had made it to the facility.

He stared at the unfolding scene for a moment.

Lawdamercy. It takes a lot a groceries to feed a gaggle this big. How they gonna do that when they ain't no town around to buy supplies and such?

§§§

CHAPTER FOURTEEN

CHATEAU LEBLANC

Eric Schmidt descended the stairs with Andre, and immediately began conversation with Augustin and Angelina near the massive fireplace in the great room, "I hope we did not keep you all waiting for too long,"

"Not at all … At least one of us has patience," replied Augustin. He grinned and gave a side look to Angelina.

As if on cue, Cyrus appeared and approached LeBlanc. "Sir, dinner is served in the dining room."

"Excellent. We shall join you directly."

Angelina reached for Eric's left arm. "Would you be so kind as to escort me?" Her green eyes sparkled.

"Wild horses could not drag me away from my duty." He smiled as their eyes met.

Augustin motioned for Eric to lead the way through the pair of walnut French doors to the formal dining room. "Believe you remember the way."

"Yes, sir, I most certainly do."

The dining table could easily seat twenty guests, but only four places were set, all on the south end. Eric led his lady friend to a seat next to the end. He pulled the gilded Louis the XIV style chair out as she slid in gracefully.

"Since there are so few of us tonight, I took the liberty of a more intimate seating arrangement as I felt it would facilitate our repartee."

Andre and Eric nodded their agreement as their host moved to the head of the table and took his seat. The two Confederate officers sat down and placed the nicely pressed linen napkins on their laps.

Eric glanced at his sweet girlfriend decked out in all her finery and then at her father with a three quarters length frock coat on. He suddenly felt slightly underdressed and somewhat self conscious.

"Mister LeBlanc, I want to apologize for our somewhat casual attire for dinner. Fact is, sir, neither of us planned to be out of uniform tonight."

He glanced across at Andre who was curious in hearing what he was going to say.

"It seems that for longer that I care to remember, all I ever wear is that same gray cavalry outfit … Day after day … week after week."

Angelina then placed her hand on his hands folded neatly in his lap. She noticed the faraway look in his eyes was one that she could not recall from their earlier meetings.

Augustin eyes misted over as he slowly shook his head. He held up a single finger, as if to signal *wait one moment.*

He rose to his feet and slowly unbuttoned his frock coat. Augustin removed it, turned around, and placed it on the back of the ornately carved armed chair.

"No, sir … It is I who needs to apologize. You and Andre are committing your lives and sacred honor to defending our homes. You and your men live outside, in the rain, heat and cold … Sleeping on the hard ground, and we civilians at home sometimes forget what sacrifices you are constantly making for our sakes."

"It is something we get used to," Andre offered.

"Understand, but I cannot comprehend living out of a saddle bag for months on end." Augustin shook his head.

Eric laughed. "Perhaps we do experience some … shall we say … challenges."

He grinned as he continued, "In fact, I only own two changes of civilian clothes … these and the buckskins I wore when I left home some sixteen months ago."

Angelina laughed and nodded. "I thought I recognized that shirt. It is the one you wore the night we first met."

"At Antoine's ... You took my heart away. How could I forget?" His blue eyes sparkled.

She blushed.

Augustin laughed. "I must say, it is much cooler without that lined linen frock."

Andre and Eric glanced at each other and laughed.

Cyrus entered with two other servants in trail, carrying a sterling silver platter with leg of lamb, another with steamed summer vegetables, and a third stacked with freshly baked rolls, hot from the oven. He placed the lamb in front of Augustin and the other dishes in front of the two guests.

"Will there be anything else, sir?" he asked after setting the platter down.

"No, thank you. My complements to the staff. It looks and smells marvelous." Augustin smiled.

Cyrus and his compatriots returned to the kitchen.

Augustin reached for Angelina's hand and extended his left toward Andre. "Would you join us in prayer?"

Eric gently clasped his girlfriend's hand as he reached across the table to take hold of Colonel Hebert's left.

Bowing his head, Augustin began saying grace. "God in heaven, thank You for this day and all the many blessings you bestow so freely to us. Thank you for the brave men who join us tonight. Guide and protect them as they serve our nation in this time of trouble.

"Place a hedge of safety around them. Thy will be done, on earth as it is in Heaven. Amen."

The others added an "Amen" as he concluded the short and somewhat solemn prayer.

"Hope you gentlemen brought your appetites with you. My chef is excellent," Augustin said.

Eric grinned. "Andre and I will attempt to do it justice. Those sprigs of rosemary give it an enticing aroma."

Angelina smiled broadly. "Do you have to cook in the field?"

Her boyfriend chuckled. "We have others to do that task, thankfully. My mother was a very good cook, but I spent most of my time learning my father's gunsmithing trade. Must say, I have learned to appreciate some of the small techniques in the culinary art, but army field kitchens do not offer much in the way of what you would call fine cuisine."

Augustin used a stag handled carving knife to slice several thin portions of lamb. "Please pass your plates. We'll be dining family style tonight. Hope you do not mind."

"Not at all," Andre replied. "It will give us some privacy to discuss some technical challenges that face Eric and me."

Augustin eyebrows raised. "Really? Something that I can help you with?"

Eric nodded. "Possibly." He leaned closer to Angelina. "Ladies, first, if you please."

She lifted her imported china plate and held it closer to the silver platter.

Her father forked a small cut of tender meat and laid it on the gold rimmed plate. "Au jus, my dear?"

"Yes, please. But only a little."

He took hold of the small silver gravy boat and poured a small amount across the roasted lamb, and she returned the plate to its place on the white linen tablecloth. "Gentlemen, do you prefer your lamb medium or medium rare?"

"Medium rare for me," Andre replied. "Plenty of au jus, if you please."

"I shall try it that way, as well," Eric added.

"A man after my own heart," Augustin said with a smile. He sliced three center cuts from the boneless leg and served them to his guests and then one for himself. "Help yourselves to the side dishes and rolls. Do not be bashful in our home."

CONFEDERATE CAMP

Bass and his two new enlisted friends waited in line as the evening meal was being ladled out from huge black cast iron cauldrons.

Richard stepped out of line to try to see what was being served. He bent over to attempt to see under the arm and past the apron of the pot bellied cook.

He stood back in with his friends. "Cain't tell fo' shore. Maybe stew, maybe chicken and dumplin's. Looks like some cornbread in those skillets."

"Sounds good to me. We did not stop for a noon meal," Michael added.

"Things, they be different in the cavalry," Bass noted. "Back home, we ate purty good, most times."

Richard shook his head. "After my daddy went and got hisself killed, things were tough for momma and us kids. She had to take in laundry and do some

NO TIME TO DIE

cooking for other folks to keep food on our table. We kids had to gather up and cut firewood to keep the wash pots boilin'."

Bass contemplated this new information. "How old was you when yore daddy died?"

"Nine … Had three little brothers and an older sister. She was eleven."

Michael, the sixteen year old, nodded. "I 'member her. She ran off and married that drummer from Tyler a couple of years ago. She was good looking, I tell you what."

Richard laughed. "Maybe so. But you oughta see her when she is expectin'." He held his hands out in front of his stomach. "Bigger 'n a whiskey barrel and mean as a snake."

Bass roared with laughter. "That mean you gonna be an uncle, don't it?"

The seventeen year old laughed. "Shoot... I already been an uncle for mor'n a year. This here one will be her number two. Took her no time at all to get in a family way, once she up and run off with that sweet talking drummer."

Bass grinned.

Michael grinned, elbowed the big black man and winked. "Told you she was a looker."

"You know that is right." Bass chuckled. "Seen that happen oncst or twice my own self. Some pretty women have a way to wrap a man 'round they little finger. Sweet little thing say, "Jump", an' he say "How high?""

Both teenage cavalrymen broke out laughing.

"That there some true fact, I swear," said Richard.

The food lines continued to move closer to the huge pots. Bass watched as a cook dipped a long handled polished steel ladle into the pot and retrieved a serving of stew. He poured it into the soldier's tin plated bowl.

Ain't nuthin' fancy but it will fill the hole.

Bass and his new friends finally reached the head of the line. Richard got his portion first and then picked a wedge shaped piece of cornbread from the portable round table.

As the Dutch ovens became empty, a cook's helper would wipe them out with a cotton rag, and quickly grease them up with a lard soaked mop, and pour in a fresh batch of cornmeal batter.

A second helper would put the rimmed lip back in place and using heavy gloves place the utensil back in the bed of smoking coals and shovel more coals onto the top of the Dutch oven.

Bass gazed upon the rows of cast iron on the strip of coals and counted the number in his head. *Twenty of them little boogers. 'Spect it take all of 'em to feed this many hongy mens.*

He took his portion of stew on his ten inch pewter plate. He picked up a slice of corn bread and set it beside the pile of mostly potatoes, carrots and celery. A couple pieces of indiscernible meat were mixed in with the vegetables and watery "gravy" thickened with corn starch.

He lifted the plate closer to his nose and tried to identify the type of protein.

Michael looked on with no little amount of amusement. "Figured it out yet, big man?"

"Figured out what?" relied Bass.

The teenagers chuckled. "Well, the great mystery, of course."

Bass' face registered the fact that he did not have a clue as to what Michael meant.

Richard edged closer as the three walked back to their encampment. "The great mystery is what is in the stew. Ain't stringy like chicken. Don't taste like pork. Beef would be tougher'n a boot if they did not cook it all day." He grinned. "That is why we call it mystery meat."

Bass laughed. "That there's a good one."

He thought for a second. "We could ask the cooks. They oughta know what went in there."

Richard shook his head. "Not a good idea. Sarge says if you complain about the food, they will make you the new cook."

Bass's eyes grew wide. "Oh, they don't want me in the kitchen. All I ever done is bring in wild game and fish ... when they was a bitin'. We had us some good cooks to make food for the whole family and all us slaves."

"They let you shoot birds, rabbits and such?" Michael's mouth was agape.

"Uh huh. Massa George, uh, I mean Captain Reeves, he let me shoot a double barrel shotgun. I shot us a big old barren doe a few days ago, and it was real good."

"Never heard the like ... Maybe Sergeant Simmons will ask the Captain to let you do some huntin' for us," Richard said. "This stew is mighty pitiful, if'n you ask me."

§§§

CHAPTER FIFTEEN

CHATEAU LEBLANC

Augustin dabbed the corners of his mouth with his linen napkin and placed in back on his lap. He glanced to Andre. "So I take it that Port Lavaca is no longer a viable seaport to handle the exportation of my cotton?"

The somber faced Cajun nodded. "As I understand it, the Federal troops took over the town in March of this year. They have posted more than a dozen warships off the Texas coast to try to intercept shipping from Houston, Galveston, and the Sabine river as well."

"The Yankees attempted a run up the Sabine, but our shore artillery batteries drove them back … at least for now," Eric added. "Down in far south Texas, in the much more sparsely populated areas, the Union Navy felt that they could take over the docks and cut off contraband shipping easier than trying to intercept every blockade runner."

"That is indeed unfortunate. Port Lavaca had a rail line connecting it with Victoria." The displeasure was evident on the plantation owner's face.

Angelina turned to Eric. "With the apparent loss of the Red River and Mississippi riverboat traffic, we had hoped to be able to transport those heavy bales of cotton by train to a port on the coast. We still have five months or so before this season's crop is in."

Eric placed a hand on hers. "We shall figure out something, my dear. Much can happen in five months."

Andre agreed. "There are very likely fifty small fishing villages along the Texas coast where a dock could be made to facilitate a commercial operation. The problem with some is the shallow depth of the Matagorda Bay waters forces a deep-draft ocean going vessel to anchor off shore and use small tenders to shuttle the cargo to the dock."

"That is burden best avoided, I should imagine," opined Eric. "How much does one of those big bales of cotton weigh?"

"Four hundred and eighty pounds ... wrapped and banded," Augustin replied.

"Whoo ... considerably more than I would have guessed." Eric's mind raced. "The tonnage can build up quickly ... If I may be so bold, may I ask how many bales you produce on a good year?"

"Each acre produces roughly one bale of finished cotton, and we have three thousand acres in cultivation," Angelina said with a smile that signaled her pride in her father's accomplishments.

"That is almost seven hundred and thirty tons," Eric replied. He looked across the table at Andre. "I understand what you meant by 'many a load of cotton from Chateau LeBlanc'."

Andre grinned. "You computed that in your head in an instant. I see why General Matson is so enamored with you."

Augustin nodded agreement. "I saw that as well. But I sense you gentlemen have more important things to discuss than my shipping challenges. Does it have anything to do with those troops that are camped between here and town?"

Eric laughed, his blue eyes sparkling. "I had intentionally avoided initiating that discussion until after dinner. It was a nice respite from the everyday focus from our daily grind."

"You earned a brief reprieve," Angelina said sweetly. "I do hope you saved room for dessert."

"And what, pray tell, is on the menu tonight?" he asked.

"Something light … Crepes Suzette with some fresh picked blackberries. They are in season, you know."

Andre's eyebrows arched as a huge smile came to his face. "One of my all time favorites."

"I, for one, am looking forward to the new experience." Eric sat up a tad straighter.

Augustin rang the small silver bell summoning the help. Cyrus and two assistants appeared and began to clear the dinner plates.

"Dessert will be served shortly, sir," Cyrus said as he cleared a few bread crumbs off the table with a C shaped silver tubular scoop. "Would you like another bottle of wine, sir?"

"No, but I believe we will have another round of cream sherry with the crepes, thank you."

"As you wish, sir."

Cryus departed the room and another servant entered with fresh silver forks for the final course.

A moment later, another returned and served the glasses of sherry.

When Cryus returned, he carried a large silver tray with four china plates of crepes. Delicate flat pastries—much thinner than pancakes—were rolled around a generous portion of Louisiana blackberries that had been lightly poached in a mixture of butter, sugar, and cinnamon. A sweet white sauce made thickened cream, sugar, flour and a hint of vanilla was drizzled on top.

He served Angelina first, then the two guests and, lastly, set the confection in front of Augustin.

"Thank you , Cyrus. That will be all."

The fifty year old man smiled, nodded but said nothing as he silently returned to the kitchen.

"Oh, my. This smells amazing," Eric said as he grinned at both his hosts.

"Bon appetite," Augustin said as he lifted his fork. "I hope it pleases you."

Angelina watched with no small amount of pleasure as Eric took the first bite. He closed his eyes and savored the flavors.

A brief flash of a memory of his mother serving dewberry cobbler on blue and white earthenware plates crossed his mind. That glorious vision almost instantly faded to the one seared into his mind — his mother's bloody body sprawled across their log cabin floor with his father laying beside her.

The smile on Angelina's face melted as she watched something overcome her young beau. His jaw tightened visibly, and a single crystal tear rolled down his left cheek and dropped to his shirt. She placed her hand on his arm and whispered, "Are you all right?"

He blinked away the tear and faked a smile. "Of course … these crepes are superb. It just that they reminded me of … uh … something."

Eric took in a deep, somewhat ragged breath and looked away for a moment—trying to regain his composure.

She saw through the bravado in an instant. Her green eyes misted over at the sight of his pain. Intuitively, she made the culinary connection. "I remember the first time we talked privately, you told me what a great cook your mother was. Does this remind you of her cobbler?"

Eric turned to her. "How did you know?"

She smiled and shrugged. "Woman's intuition … It's only been a little over a year. It is completely natural for you to still feel the pain."

Eric nodded. "I know … I … uh … just try so hard not to let it show." He took another forkful of the crepes and savored it.

Andre had watched the exchange and knew full well what the younger man had gone through. "My compliment to the chef, Augustin. This, my friend, is as good as my wife's best, and she is quite well known in Natchitoches for her pastry."

"I shall pass the kind words to my staff."

Shortly after they finished dessert, Augustin suggested that the four move to the study to finish their conversation.

He seated his daughter and her beau in a fabric covered settee placed near the east-facing window —he motioned to Andre to have a seat in one of two matching armchairs covered in burgundy colored leather.

"I have been thinking about your troops camped in the pastures nearby. Shreveport surely cannot be their destination."

Eric glanced to Andre.

The affable Cajun smiled. "Your conclusion is correct my friend. Colonel Schmidt had been tasked to get them across the mighty Mississippi."

Angelina gasped slightly and squeezed Eric's hand.

He patted the back of her hand gently. "It is all right, my dear. I drafted our friend Andre as my maritime consultant. Staff your weaknesses, as Sun Tzu would counsel."

Augustin stroked his chin as his forehead furrowed. "Please tell me that you will not try to cross at Vicksburg."

Eric chuckled. "I will gladly report that I have absolutely no interest in challenging the Union Navy." He looked at Angelina, smiled and winked.

"Sir, we will not divulge when and where we plan to cross the big muddy ... to do so could possibly put both of your lives in danger. That information would be sensitive to military operational secrecy," Andre said.

Augustin nodded. "I understand ... Are you planning to pilot a steamboat across?"

Andre shook his head. "Oh, no. It would take several round trips ... and the mouths of the Arkansas and Red Rivers are effectively blockaded with Union gunboats."

Eric turned to face Angelina's father. "My plan, in its current iteration is to construct a large flattop ferry. We will be needing to acquire a portable steam powered sawmill."

Augustin nodded. "Simple enough ... I could loan you mine. We built the warehouses and workers quarters using one. It sits idle most of the year."

"Very generous offer, sir, but I could pay you for its purchase."

The wealthy planter shook his head. "Not necessary, young man. However, I would prefer to have it returned, if possible. One cannot always acquire finely machined items like a steam engine in these trying times."

Andre nodded. "We all have seen the effects of the embargo. Our next challenge will be sufficient cable to rig a ferry."

"But is not the Mississippi over a mile wide in some places?" Angelina's face reflected her concern.

"Yes, but not everywhere," Eric responded. "We have picked out a spot that will make the task easier."

Augustin sat silent for a moment as he gathered his thoughts. "Have you considered a chain barge? A steam engine can drive a worm gear pull the chain through a capstan. It is similar to what large vessels use to hoist and lower their anchors."

Eric shook his head. He glanced to Andre and shrugged. "I am not familiar with a chain capstan. That is a new one on me."

The Cajun grinned. "Relax, Colonel. I am intimately familiar with them. Augustin makes a good point. Cables are notoriously slick, hard to

deal with, and blacksmiths hammer welding them together in the woods is fraught with serious concerns. I will share what I know about chains …
"

§§§

CHAPTER SIXTEEN

CONFEDERATE CAMP

Captain Reeves stepped into the opening in the canvas tent and looked at Bass seated cross legged on his bed roll. "I take it you got something to eat."

"Yassah. It filled the hole, if'n you knows what I mean."

George nodded. "I am afraid we were spoiled with Miss Martha's cooking. She has a way with soups and stews."

Bass grinned. "That she does, Massa, that she does. Must be them little green things she puts in from the garden. She chops 'em up fine and put 'em lotsa things ... even her scrambled eggs."

"You are referring to herbs ... such as sage, rosemary, and thyme."

"Time? Is that there is one of them herb things?"

"Different kind of thyme. Sounds the same but are spelled..." He shook his head. "Never mind that ... Do we have anything to write on?"

Bass shrugged and shook his head.

"Of course not." George thought for a moment. "If things permit, I shall go into town tomorrow and see if I cannot acquire a traveling secretary."

The confused look on Bass' face conveyed his utter bafflement.

"It is not a person, Bass. A portable writing device ... also known as a lap desk."

None of those terms meant a thing to a person denied the ability to learn to read or write.

"Forget it. Help me out of these infernal boots. They are not quite broken in." He held his right foot out to the muscular slave as he steadied himself on the central pole of the tent.

Bass placed his callused right hand on the tip of the squared toed knee-high boot. His left grabbed the heel and with a quick tug with his left hand and a push on the other, the boot came off smoothly.

The major gave a sigh of relief. He transferred his weight to the foot with a sweaty woolen sock and repeated the process before taking a seat on the cot. "Ahh. Much better." He removed his damp socks and rubbed his feet.

He glanced at his cavalry boots. "They should fit perfectly in a few more days. See if you can get them shined up before reveille in the morning."

"Yassah." Bass dug into his master's saddle bags for a small circular tin of black shoe polish and a discolored cotton cloth.

CHATEAU LEBLANC

Augustin looked at Eric and grinned. "Three thousand feet of two inch chain? It would be a major miracle to find such a thing in Shreveport. You might have to travel to Dallas, Marshall, or perhaps even Houston by train to make such an acquisition."

"That thought crossed my mind … Plus a chain capstan, pulleys, gears to reverse direction and a pair of wide leather drive bands to transfer power from a steam engine to run the barge." His brow furrowed slightly.

The elder LeBlanc sat back, crossed his arms and smiled. "You will get it done, I am certain of that. However, it will be done tomorrow. I would like some time to ask Andre a few more questions regarding getting our cotton to market. My dear, would you like to take Eric out and inspect the docks?"

"But, Father …." His suggestion caught her off guard. Eric had been shown the Red River docks on his previous visit.

Augustin's hint was aimed at providing the two lovers a bit of privacy. Her green eyes sparkled when that simple realization became apparent.

"That is a wonderful idea, Father. I will have Cyrus prepare a lantern."

Eric pushed back from the table and got to his feet. "By your leave, gentlemen." He gently pulled the chair from beneath Angelina as she gracefully arose.

"We must be on the lookout for water moccasins," the lanky Texan said as he descended the steps leading to the river front landing.

"Would they not be asleep by this time of night?

"Seriously doubt it … It is too hot during the day for them to be out in the sun … Them being cold blooded creatures and all."

The pair stepped onto the wide cypress planks of the wide walkway leading to the T shaped docks. Angelina saw nothing threatening in the feeble light of the coal oil lantern. She came to an abrupt halt on the open walkway and spun Eric around. A mischievous smile cross her face. "Those snakes may be cold blooded, but I am not."

She pulled his face to her and kissed him passionately.

He knelt down slightly and set the lantern down. His callused hands wrapped around her hourglass waist as he pulled her tightly to him.

Her scent was intoxicating to him. The two kissed for a full minute until they broke away and each took in a ragged breath.

Angelina laughed. Her green eyes sparkled like tiny diamonds in the pale light of the lantern.

"God, you are so beautiful," Eric said.

"And you, sir, are more handsome than I dared remember. I cannot believe that we did it again."

His face reflected his momentary confusion. "Did what again, pray tell?"

"Forgot to breathe." Angelina pulled his face to hers and devoured the taste of his lips once again. "Do you know how much I missed you?"

He chuckled. "I am starting to get the idea." He slipped one hand up her back and into her flowing red tresses. Gently, he cupped the back of her petite head and held her tight.

After a full two minutes of a long, lingering kiss, Angelina giggled.

"What? Did I do something wrong?" he asked.

"Of course not, silly. It's just that your mustache … it tickles a little bit."

Eric pulled back slightly. "I can shave it off if you prefer … "

She shook her head and reached up for the flared tips of the big man's blond handlebar mustache and grinned. "I rather fancy it. It gives you a certain …

cavalier look. More debonair, I should think." She pulled his face to hers.

He chuckled as they kissed again.

She broke off the kiss. "What is it you find funny?"

He smiled as his eyes devoured her beauty again and again. "No one has ever called me debonair before … I doubt my father even knew what that word means."

Angelina sighed. "If he could see you now, he would know. My God, you are even more handsome than you were last summer."

Eric gently took her by the hand. He stooped down, grabbed the polished steel hoop attached to the lantern and picked it up.

He led her a few feet to the bench seat on the back side of the docks. After carefully checking for unwanted serpentine interlopers, he lifted her hand and slow spun her around in a theatrical fashion. "Won't you have a seat, milady?"

"Why, yes, I believe I will." Angelina curtsied, and gracefully sat down.

Eric placed the coal oil lantern about ten feet from where she sat and slid it under the bench— making it much darker except for a semi-circle of yellow light cast across the cypress planks of the seldom used wharf.

"Much better," he said as he gazed up at the stars. He settled down beside her. "Remember the first night we sat here?"

"I think about it often. You knew so much about the stars and planets."

He laughed. "Learned a lot more being outside almost every night since then. Actually, we try not to move too much at night, but when we have to, it certainly helps to be able to navigate in the right direction."

"Sounds dangerous ... are you ever scared?"

"No so much for me. I do worry about the men that serve with me." His face took on a somber look.

"Many of them are like brothers I never had." He turned away for a moment and took in a deep breath. "Enough of that, if you do not mind. I would like to concentrate on us."

She smiled as the sparkle returned to his eyes. In the pale light, his sky blue eyes took on a darker cerulean color. "I understand ... at least I think I do. I love the way you said *us*."

"For this minute, this hour … however long we have together … let the rest of the world take care of itself. I just want to hold you."

She reached out and held on tightly as he wrapped his muscular arms around her. *I have never felt so close to another man like I do when I am with him.*

After a full minute or two, Angelina lifted her head from his chest. "I can hear your heart beating."

"Certainly hope so. I hear bad things happen when it stops." He winked at her in the near darkness.

"I am trying to be serious." She pouted, sticking her lower lip out slightly.

Eric laughed. "You cannot be mad at me. I was merely trying to make you laugh."

The fake pout disappeared as quickly as it had come. "I have to tell you what I am feeling right this minute. When I was listening to your heart, it felt like we were … "

"One person? Melting together … no you, no me, just us?"

Angelina's green eyes were rimmed with tears of joy. "You felt it, too!" She slipped her arms from around his chest and pulled his face to hers again.

They smothered each other with tiny butterfly kisses as the crickets, whippoorwills and bullfrogs serenaded the young lovers on the banks of the Red River.

A brilliant meteor crossed the clear night sky overhead and exploded into a dozen smaller ones—each leaving a small visible trail of smoke barely discernible in the moonlight.

Eric caught sight of the phenomenon out of the corner of his eye, He gently lifted her chin up and pointed. "Do you believe in signs?"

The beautiful red head nodded and smiled. "I believe what I read in scripture ... believe God brought you to me."

His face radiated his love and joy. He held her close and whispered, "I do, too."

§§§

CHAPTER SEVENTEEN

ARKADELPHIA, ARKANSAS

It was eleven minutes past two in the sultry heat of mid July when the first elements of the huge military convoy came into view just outside the little town. Major Doran Ingrham grinned as he recognized the outlines of a pair of familiar riders near the front.

He turned to a senior enlisted man. "Speak of the devil. They made good time. 'Spect you can ride back to the park and have the boys saddle up."

"Yes, sir. Reckon our little vacation is officially over." He wheeled his steeldust mare around and quickly brought her to a road trot. Tiny puffs of red dust rose up from each hoofbeat on the sunbaked Arkansas roadway.

Doran squeezed his calves against his sorrel gelding. The well-disciplined but spirited horse responded by prancing out and smoothly picked up a rocking horse lope to close the one hundred fifty yard distance to the approaching columns.

Ingrham reined the pony beside the lead element, came to a halt, and spun around to match the speed of the other volunteers from Texas. He snapped a salute to Eric and nodded at the other officers. "Good to see you, Colonel. Looks like you are bringin' half of Texas with you."

Eric return the salute and extended his hand. "Almost ... have one brigade of cavalry and another of mounted infantry. Plus supplies and everything we think we shall need to cross over the Big Muddy. I want you to meet Colonel Theodore

Armstrong. He is commanding the Seventh Cavalry Brigade."

"Howdy, Colonel. Pleased to make your acquaintance. I am Doran Inghram, from a little place you never heard of out in West Texas." Doran raised a hand to wave at the officer riding inside of Eric at the front of the regiment.

"Your commander speaks highly of you, Major Ingrham. I have heard a West Texas drawl a few times before." He grinned. "He tells me you are a wonder at training horses."

"Have been thrown off one or two, if that what you mean, sir."

"Methinks you are too modest, Doran. Eric says that you trained his horse to lie down on command and allow a soldier to shoot over him. Were you in the cavalry before the war?"

"No sir … Did a stretch with the Texas Rangers. Fought me a fight or two with Comanches." He glanced at Eric. "Now, them there are a bunch o' light cavalry cutthroats that you most assuredly do not want to give an edge to … Trust me."

"My man here learned a trick or two from his narrow escapes. He would be an excellent asset for your junior officers and senior enlisted to spend some time with." Eric grinned before he continued.

"We always take the opportunity to get together and plan our next moves. While those Yankees are not exactly like the Texas plains Indians, a well executed ambush is still a great ambush. I respect the way the major thinks."

Colonel Armstrong nodded. "As I understand it, we will have several days preparation moving into position and building the ferry and barge on site. Perhaps you can be available to help train our mounts and give us the benefit of your experience in such matters."

Doran locked eyes with the younger colonel. Eric simply gave him a single nod. The wiry forty year old from West Texas removed his cavalry hat and wiped the sweat from his brow with a paisley print brown cotton bandanna he kept tucked under his tunic collar.

He shook his head, allowing the long silver ponytail he sported to shake free. "Someday, I might get used to the humidity we have run into in this part of the country. It gets real hot out in the Big Bend, but compared to this, it was a dry heat." He chuckled as he tugged his sweaty hat into place.

"Colonel Armstrong, looks like my colonel has done given me my marchin' orders …Be right proud to help educate some of your sergeants in the way I learned to train horses. If y'all can pick, say … maybe three men per company … I can show them what they need to know."

"I shall see that it happens," Armstrong replied.

Eric nodded his agreement. "We will be camping tonight in Tulip. Sent word ahead and had most of my regiment redeploy there and set up a campsite for tonight. Your men will be fed by my staff cooks."

Armstrong looks a bit surprised at the information. "I had assumed that we would be staying over near Arkadelphia."

Eric shook his head. "That would put us four hours father away from our destination. Our overnight in Tulip will be short. We will break camp at first light, and have a combat breakfast of coffee, bacon, beans, and corn dodgers. Your men will not even unload their wagons.

"By noon, we should have your regiments up to the Arkansas River ferry crossing. My logistic support team will break down the Tulip camp and join up with us before the last of the Twelth Mounted Infantry is across … if all goes to plan."

"Must say, you operate a bit differently than I am used to," Colonel Armstrong said.

Eric grinned and glanced over to Doran. "Have been told that a time or two."

The column approached a fork in the road. The city of Arkadelphia lay straight ahead. A small clapboard sign painted with an arrow pointing to the right and the words *Tulip*, and *Pine Bluff* was staked on the right side of the road.

Colonel Schmidt pointed down the cutoff "Gentlemen, we are going to take the road to Tulip. Ted, when we get up to the road from Arkadelphia to Pine Bluff, we will rendezvous with men from my Third Company. At that point, they will provide security for the supply wagons of both regiments. You and I will take the mounted troops at a full road trot the sixteen miles to Tulip."

"You say there is already a camp set up for them there?"

"That is exactly right. A detachment from Arkansas volunteers has been set up there to block the Yankees who have taken over Pine Bluff. I want to get your men and, more importantly, their mounts in shape to be able to move long distances quickly."

Eric made sure that Colonel Armstrong understood exactly his point. The seasoned officer was looking him in the eyes as he said. "Once we leave Tulip, we are essentially entering enemy held territory."

Commander of the First Company—Major Billy White—rode alongside the two colonels. His eyes narrowed as he listened in. "Excuse me, gentlemen, if I may interrupt ... Are you saying we might have to fight our way to the Mississippi?"

Eric shook his head. "Certainly hope not ... Not my plan. We bloodied their nose pretty well ten days ago on that train derailment. There was basically no way for them to catch up with us because of the vast distances involved ... That and the fact that my men and I move quickly."

"I see why you are interested in whipping our regiment into top physical condition. Capital idea, Colonel," replied Major White.

Doran chuckled. "We delivered all those Yankee prisoners of war down to Texarkana and came back in here in only two days. Colonel Schmidt gave our boys some rest time after that to heal our wounded and get ready for this next operation. We have been eating pretty high on the hog with the Yankee rations we captured."

Eric playfully backhanded the wiry major across the midsection. "Yeah, I thought you looked like you were starting to put on a little weight."

"And you are so hilarious, Colonel. Have you ever thought about startin' your own travelin' show?" Doran shot him a side look.

Eric grinned and winked at him. "Hold your fire, amigo ... thought I already did."

Bass Reeves rode alongside the men of his master's Second Company. Captain George Reeves did not wish to have a repeat of the experience in Shreveport where the two were separated in the move from the railway station.

A pair of riders from the front of the column rode back to the lead elements of the Second. Bass recognized only one of them—the Seventh Regiment Sergeant Major. He listened carefully as the man called out orders.

"A mile up this cut off, we will separate from the freight wagons and proceed at a road trot to tonight's encampment. The distance is sixteen miles. Security for the wagons will be provided by units of the Second Regiment from Texas." He pointed a thumb at Major Ingrham. "Any Questions?"

"No, Sergeant Major. I understand," replied Captain Reeves.

"Very good, sir. Carry on."

Bass watched as the two men reined south and repeated the same message again to the Third Company. *Wonder what that is all about? These army men shore do things funny.*

Fifteen minutes later, the convoy turned onto the main road from Arkadephia to Tulip and Pine Bluff.

Bass saw a company sized group of riders in a field, waiting for the mounted cavalry to pass. The captain in charge of the security detail saluted Captain Reeves.

The regiment Sergeant Major and Major Ingrham galloped past the Second Company and continued to the front of the half-mile long column. Bass heard the sound of a bugle call from the First Company. It was repeated by a bugler riding next to his master.

He turned and looked back as he heard the same notes being played behind him.

Major White yelled out his orders over his left shoulder loud and clear, "First Company ... Forward at a trot ... ho!"

One hundred and three mounted cavalry simultaneously spurred their horses onward. At first, the unit's movement was ragged, but after a few seconds, the group settled down to a rapid pace that was easy on the animals and ate up the road miles.

Bass felt his pulse quicken as Captain Reeves called out and repeated the order. He wore no spurs, but kicked his heels lightly into the sorrel's flanks.

It was not really needed as Whiskey responded to his inbred herd instinct when all the other ponies broke into a rapid trot.

Bass was not sure why, but suddenly he felt like he was a member of the Second Company, and not just a slave to its commander.

Bass was happy to see the campsite on the outskirts of Tulip come into view. His thigh muscles were aching, and he felt that a blister was starting to form on his right calf where his boot rubbed against the brass buckle in his stirrup hanger.

Major White raised a gloved hand and called out "Forward at walk, ho!" The lead elements of the First Company reined back, allowing the slightly strung out column of cavalry to collapse into a more parade like procession.

The Second and Third Company as well as the three from the mounted infantry regiment snaked into position behind them.

Colonel Schmidt reined right and brought Thunder to a halt. He watched closely as the first two companies passed, and then wheeled about and trotted to pull aside Colonel Armstrong.

"How do they look?" the senior officer asked.

"About what I expected. A quarter of the mounts are lathered up a bit ... not quite in shape for extended combat operations. I will have some my men show your new soldiers how to cool them off, and rub them down properly, with your permission."

"I appreciate your assistance in that matter. As you know, many of my men are brand new volunteers. We have been attempting to cover the basics of military discipline, military commands, and rudimentary cavalry maneuvers. We have a long ways to go."

Eric laughed. "I can most certainly relate, sir. I, myself, was green as the proverbial gourd in March of last year. Fortunately, I teamed up with a West Point mentor who pushed me as hard as he thought prudent."

Ted nodded. "General Matson is quite capable. But you, sir, are an exceptional officer, if I do say so myself."

"Appreciate the complement, sir … However, I defer the accolades to my men." Eric turned to Major Ingrham. "Doran can you walk the regiments on a cool down, and then dismiss them to tend to the horses? We still have plenty of daylight to set up the tents and get these men fed."

"As you wish, Colonel." He called over to Major White. "Sir can you lead your company in a large left hand circle between here and the tree line?" He pointed north to a tall stand of pine trees. "We need to left the mounts cool down properly, or they won't be worth a tinker's damn in the morning."

"That we can do, sir. First Sergeant, you heard the man."

§§§

CHAPTER EIGHTEEN

CONFEDERATE CAMP
TULIP, ARKANSAS

Bass was dismayed to see the column veer to the left. *Maybe this is not the right camp we be headed to.* He allowed himself to settle down in the saddle to ease the incipient cramps forming in his inner thighs. *Ooh ... that smarts a bit.*

His bottom was bruised by the jarring of the extended road trot. He was familiar with riding, of course, but most of his experience was on the backs of a pair of plantation mules, and he never had ridden anywhere dusk to dawn, day after day.

Bass watched with interest as three riders broke off from the turning column and headed into the Confederate camp.

Captain George Reeves looked at the sun still rather high in the cloudless western sky. He lifted his kepi and wiped the sweat from his brow. Both of his ears were burnt from the steady exposure to the July sun. He glanced over at Bass wearing a broad brimmed hat. *Lucky man. Probably never had a sunburn in his life, I would wager. I wonder if I should have asked for the other style of head gear.*

He dismissed the thoughts concerning his uniform choices as he watched the column continue to curve left. *Must be letting the ponies cool down, if that is even a possibility in this blasted heat.*

Twenty minutes later, the two regiments were dismissed to unsaddle their horses, and tie them to long picket lines. The horses began to graze the brown sun-baked forage, and the riders stowed their saddles and soogans nearby.

Doran and a dozen other cavalrymen from the Second Brigade walked through the camp, showing the new recruits how to rub down their mounts with curry brushes or handfuls of straw.

"One thing I want you boys to burn into your brain is that pony is your ticket both to and from a battle. The better you treat it, the better it will perform when the chips are down. Next to your weapon, that horse is the most important thing you own." There was not a hint of joking in the lanky Texan's drawl.

Bass watched closely and tried to follow the man's instruction to the letter. He had two horses in his care, as Captain Reeves had left him and headed off to find out where his personal campsite would be. Bass knelt down to grab another handful of dry grass.

A cramp came upon him as he tried to stand back up. He grimaced and kneaded his left inner thigh as he hopped around in a little circle.

Doran caught sight of his distress and stepped closer to hold onto his shoulder. "You all right there, cowboy?"

Bass reached out and grabbed Doran's right hand for balance as he lifted his left leg and squeezed the muscle tightly. "Jest a cramp, Mister. Been fightin' 'em off for a half hour or so."

"Bet your ol' butt is raw as hell, too ... First time for a long trot?" Doran grinned.

"Yassah. How you know that?"

"Well, let me say that I spent more years in the saddle than most. Let me show you something."

Bass looked at him somewhat askance.

Doran held on to Bass' hand. "Gonna have to trust me on this. Put your left foot down and lean over this way ... lean into me. Stretch out that inner thigh muscle that is tying you up in knots. Easy now."

Bass was breathing somewhat ragged as the pain sharply flared and slowly subsided in his thigh as the muscle gradually stopped cramping. He made eye contact with Doran and smiled wanly. "Thank you, mister. 'Preciate it a whole bunch."

Doran helped pull the bigger man erect. "Any time. You probably need to do the same thing on the right side as well."

Bass nodded. "Uh huh. They both been powerful sore."

Doran held on as Bass leaned to his left, stretching out the inner thigh muscle.

"Ooh, that do be actin' like it's mad at me." Bass gritted his teeth.

"It does, but now you know how to take care of it." Doran looked over the two horses Bass was rubbing down. "Nice conformation. Good breeding. How long have you had them?"

"They ain't mine ... Massa Reeves ... uh, mean to say Captain Reeves, uh, he raised them on his pappy's plantation over by Sherman in Grayson County."

Doran raised his eyebrows. "I see. You are Captain Reeves' ... aide."

Bass nodded.

"If you like, I can stop by in a while and bring you some liniment for that backside of yours. We have another full day in the saddle tomorrow. I would be happy to teach you some riding techniques that will make it a whole lot more comfortable for you."

The big man smiled broadly. "Mister if'n you can teach me that, you be sent straight from heaven. I thought I done knew how to ride ... Seems like maybe I don't."

The silver haired major laughed. "Nobody ever mistook me for an angel, that is for certain. But I hate to see a good man in pain … 'Specially if a helpful hint can prevent it. Tell you what … You finish rubbing these horses down, and I will stop by and see you before dinner. What outfit are you with?"

Bass' face relayed his momentary confusion. "My master, he be in charge of the Second Company, but as fo' me … uh, I ain't 'xactly in the army … 'xactly."

"I understand." Doran stuck out his hand. "I am Major Doran Ingrham. What is you name?"

"Reeves. They call me Bass Reeves. Pleased to meet you, sir." He took hold of the major's hand—his massive one dwarfing the slender Texan's.

"Pleased to meet you as well." Doran turned to walk away but spun around as he remembered something else. He held up a single index finger. "One more thing … Salt … Ask the cook for extra salt tonight. You have been sweatin' a lot in all this heat and a little extra salt will help you with those leg cramps."

"Yassah. Salt … be askin' 'em for it." Bass watched as Doran moved to the next group of soldiers tending their mounts.

Bass finished rubbing down both horses and headed toward the busier part of the camp. He found Captain Reeves in a discussion with his company First Sergeant. He waited for a couple minutes as they discussed the evening meal schedule.

"I do not comprehend why they have our regiment set up for dinner at seventeen hundred hours." George looked at his pocket watch. "That is only forty minutes from now. They do not even have a mess tent up."

The NCO shook his head. "It certainly not the way I would have done it. At least the men have their pup tents erected." He pointed at the rows of low canvas shelters set up in long neat lines.

"Every one but me," the captain grumbled. He turned to see Bass standing mutely nearby. "When are you going to get my tent set up?"

"As soon as they gets here with them wagons, Massa. We ain't gots us a little tent like they do. It be all folded up neat and proper in the wagon."

"Of course it is. You be ready to get it up as soon as it gets here."

"Yassah. I do that." He looked over at the rows of cooking kettles set up for Colonel Schmidt's regiment. He gazed at the size of the camp extending to the east.

On a impulse, he offered a comment to his master. "Captain Reeves, mind I knows why we gonna eat early tonight."

George looked at him and then glanced at his NCO and grinned. "Do tell us why we are scheduled to eat at seventeen hundred. I would love to hear your analysis of the situation."

Bass shrugged. "Y'all can take it or leave it, but I been doing some figgerin' … We gots three hundred cavalry men. That other bunch of horse soldiers with us is a 'nuther three hundred. They be 'bout three hundred more that was already done here 'afore we gots here. That be close to nine hundred mens all told."

George glared at him. "So you can add. What is your point?"

Bass looked down and then back at him. "Wellsah, our cooks ain't gonna get here 'till it be near dark and they ain't gonna be able to cook nothin', cause they ain't even got a fire started. Maybe them cooks over yonder cain't feed nine hundred folks all at onest." Bass pointed over to the men of the Second Cavalry and then shrugged.

The First Sergeant considered what Bass said and nodded. "Man's got a point there. Splittin' up the unit creates some interesting logistical challenges."

Captain Reeves thought for a second and nodded. "Perhaps you are right, Bass. That is a good point. In the meantime, bring our bed rolls and saddle bags over here." He pointed to an empty spot where he wanted to erect his tent.

"Get some men when the wagons arrive and get us set up here. The Colonel told me some things will not be done as usual, so most of the supply wagons will not even be unloaded."

Bass nodded. "I understands. I be ready, Major." He turned and headed back to the picket line where his and his master's saddles were stashed.

He anxiously scanned the dirt road back toward Arkadelphia, but the anticipated wagon train was still nowhere in sight.

Reaching the stored tack, he carefully knelt down and began to untie the latigo straps holding the saddlebags. He looked around and saw that no one was paying him a bit of attention.

Bass unbuckled his left bag and removed a small wrinkled paper sack. He carefully opened it and peered inside. Counting the pieces twice, he came up with a total of five—including a roll of Neccos, two Turkish delights and two peppermint sticks.

Lawd a mercy. They ain't much left of what that Mister Farmer sold me. He pondered for a full minute before he unrolled the Neccos. He carefully pealed off a single dime sized disk and slipped it in his mouth. He savored the flavor and closed his eyes. For a moment, he was back in Sherman, Texas.

§§§

CHAPTER NINETEEN

TULIP, ARKANSAS

The Union spy gazed out of the second story window of Mrs. Winter's Boarding House at the extensive convoy of Confederate freight wagons approaching the rapidly growing camp. He held a note pad in his hands where he kept a tally of the number of teams involved and what type of visible freight he could identify.

Two of the wagons were completely covered with tan canvas tarps. One had a team of four horses, the other only a pair. He sat the note pad down on a small writing desk and picked up a pair of binoculars to get a better look at the cargo.

Master Sergeant Woody Williams, head of the security detail escorting the wagon train, kept his eyes scanning the countryside. With the sun as his back, he rode beside the second wagon while allowing his cavalry company to spread out on both sides, in front of and behind the slow moving freight haulers.

He glanced at a two story white clapboard house with a picket fence in the front yard. It was sited some sixty yards off the road and almost a half mile from the main part of the small town.

A bright flash caught his eyes as the summer sun reflected off of something in one of the upstairs windows. Woody could tell it was not just the sun bouncing off the window pane, as the flash was noticeably much smaller and centered in the opening.

Woody knew exactly what sunlight's reflection from a pair of binoculars should look like. Colonel Schmidt had made sure every man in the regiment had the opportunity to look though his pair of captured optics and also see what telltale signal they could give away if the user was not careful.

Master Sergeant Williams did not know who was watching them arrive, but he sure as shooting was going to find out. He brought his mount up to a slow lope and pulled up alongside his staff sergeant.

"Murphy, you got command from here in. Tell the Lieutenant pulling up the rear that I had urgent business with Major Ingrham, if he asks where I went."

"You got it, Woody. Did you see somebody eyeballin' us from the two story house?" He tilted his head in that direction.

Williams grinned. "Least while I know I was not making it up. Just act like everything is normal. Maybe we can catch 'em."

Murphy nodded.

Woody nudged his bay gelding into a road trot. He kept his head swiveling around but made sure his scan took in the suspect house on every sweep of the area.

He caught sight of his commanding officer standing next to a pair of men. He headed that way.

Colonel Schmidt took a piece of crusty white bread and sopped up the last of the beef gravy on his pewter plate. He bit off the end and enjoyed the flavors and lastly popped the end piece in his mouth. Using the back of his hand, he wiped the tiny smudge of gravy off his bushy blonde mustache.

Bass Reeves finished off the ear of corn, freshly harvested from a nearby farmer's field. It was dripping in butter and loaded down with pepper and extra salt. "Y'all's cooks could surely teach them boys in our regiment a thing or two 'bout victuals."

Doran laughed. "It is not always like this, trust me. This canned beef is courtesy the US Army." He grinned. "Special appropriation ... way up north of Little Rock."

"I does not rightly know what that word means," Bass said with a puzzled look.

Eric grinned as he looked over at the big black man. "It means we took it from them. Derailed a Yankee supply train and carried off their food."

Bass nodded. "Appreciate the good eatin'. Jest wanted to thank you again for that liniment, Major. My pore ol' backside feels better all ready."

"That is a good thing," Doran said. " Remember what I said ... do not get that stuff of your privates. It will light 'em up like a house on fire. Guaranteed." He chuckled.

"Spoken like a man with experience." Eric laughed.

Master Sergeant Williams rode up. He dismounted and dropped the reins. His horse never moved. "Colonel, got something important to discuss with you."

"Sure, Woody. What is it?"

Williams looked Bass up and down. He didn't recognize the big black man in overalls. "Sir, it is a security matter." He tilted his head away from the other men.

"Understand." He turned to Bass and Doran. "Excuse me, gentleman." Eric walked a few yards away. "What is the situation?"

Doran eyed the two soldiers discussing the matter with great interest. He watched as Williams pointed toward the distant house. Eric spoke a few words to the sergeant, he nodded, and said something back. With a sense of urgency, Woody grabbed his horse's reins and swung into the saddle.

He wheeled left and spurred the steeldust mare into a full gallop between two long lines of tents.

Bass heard the man call out "Comin' through" to get the attention of the soldiers milling about. Startled troops scattered to the side to give way to a man on a mission.

Eric approached with a solemn look on his face. "Saddle up. We have a job to do."

Doran reached out and took the pewter plate from his hand. He passed it, along with his own, to Bass. "Hold on to these, would you?"

"Yassah. I takes care of 'em fo' you."

Eric strode for the picket line of the Second Regiment.

Doran had to hustle to match the taller man's gait. "What is going on?"

He turned and spoke in a low voice, without breaking stride. "Woody thinks he located a Union spy. I sent him on a roundabout path back to the house. He will detain anyone who tries to leave."

"And we are going inside, I take it."

"Yep. Just you and I."

"This will be interesting." A wry grin came to the major's face.

MRS. WINTERS BOARDING HOUSE

Eloise Winters—recently widowed when her husband Nathan was killed in fighting during the fall of Little Rock—was interrupted by the knock on her front door.

She wiped the flour dust off her hands on the cotton apron protecting a blue Gingham print dress and headed for the main entrance. She was surprised to see two horses outside the picket fence and opened the nine paneled oak door.

The sight of two uniformed Confederate officers made her gasp. The color drained from her face. "Oh no … Lord do not let it be my boys."

It took a second for Eric to realize what their visit could look like to a woman who probably had family serving in the war.

He held up his hand. "No Ma'am. We are not from mortuary services. I am Colonel Eric Schmidt, Commander of the Second Cavalry regiment from Texas. Major Ingrham here is my Executive Officer."

Eloise allowed herself to breathe. "Thank you, Jesus. You see, I lost my dear husband Nathan in the fighting up in Little Rock a few months back." Her eyes teared up.

Eric reached out his hand. "My deepest condolences for your loss, Ma'am. I regret any pain our visit may have engendered. I assure you it was unintended."

She grasped his hand with both of hers. "Thank you, Colonel. I shall be fine in a moment." She sniffed back a bit of drainage from the tears. "Were you two gentlemen interested in accommodations?"

Eric shook his head. "No, Ma'am. We have an important matter that we need to discuss with you. May we come inside?"

Sergeant Williams rode in from the woods overlooking the north side and back of the house.

He ground tied his mare and entered the yard through the picket fence gate.

Mrs. Winters' face displayed her confusion. She glanced past Doran at Woody coming up the walk.

"He is with us, Ma'am," Ingrham said.

"Where are my manners? Of course you gentlemen are welcome inside." She stepped aside and pulled the door open wider for the three men to enter. Once everyone was inside she closed the door. "It is another hot one today, is it not?"

She smiled. "I suppose that is nothing new for you fighting men."

"No, Ma'am," Eric replied. "May we ask you a few questions?"

"Of course," she said as she wiped off her hands once more on her apron. "I am Mrs. Nathan Winter, owner of this home. Have begun taking in boarders to make ends meet in the past few weeks. You may call me Eloise."

Eric smiled. "As you wish, Ma'am … Eloise, have you or any of you family members been upstairs in the last ten minutes?"

She laughed. "Heavens, no. I have been in the kitchen for the past hour, trying to get dinner ready at six. My daughter is married now and lives down in Texarkana. My two sons are off serving in the artillery."

"I see," Eric continued. "Do you have any boarders upstairs at this time?"

"Just Mister Taylor. He has been feeling poorly this week and has stayed in his room for the past two days."

Doran's eyebrow raised at the new information. "Can you tell us much about him?"

She nodded. "He is very polite. He's a traveling salesman, you know ... and he paid cash up front."

"Is he, by any chance, staying in the southwest corner room of the second floor?" Woody asked.

"Why, yes, he is. How did you know that?" Eloise asked.

"Lucky guess," Woody replied.

"We would like to talk to him, in private, if you do not mind." The look on Colonel Schmidt's face was serious. Dead serious. "Woody, would you please keep Mrs. Winters company? We should not be too long."

"Yes, sir."

Eloise had a dozen questions on the tip of her tongue but kept silent as the two officers slowly ascended the carpeted stairwell. She noticed with more than a little apprehension that each of the men unlatched the flaps on their side arm holsters.

"Did he do something wrong?" she asked the sergeant in a low voice.

"Ma'am, to tell you the truth, I do know for certain ... We have to be kinda particular in the performance of our duties, 'cause so many lives are at stake."

Woody motioned to the Chippendale couch covered in a polished cotton chintz fabric. "Why do not you sit down and take a little break? They will be back down in a few minutes."

"Will you join me?" She sat down into position and smoothed the apron over her knees.

"To tell the truth, Ma'am, I have been in the saddle almost all day. These here pants is real dusty, and kinda wet with sweat."

He felt the back of his pants. "It feels purty darn good to be standing up for a little while, but thank you kindly for your hospitality."

Eric and Doran toe–heeled down the heart of pine wood hallway. Twelve feet from the end of the passageway were two doors on either side. The entrance on the right was obviously the one to the corner bedroom from which the reflection came.

Eric pulled the 1858 Remington .44 from his holster. He thumbed the hammer back silently to full cock.

He pointed at Doran and then at the polished brass door knob.

The wiry major nodded and used his left hand to grasp the handle. As he drew his Colt from his own holster, he slowly turned the knob to quietly clear the dead bolt from the jamb.

Eric held his breath in anticipation. He could feel his heart pounding his temples.

Doran shot a sideways glance at the young colonel, and nodded affirmation that the door was now unlocked and ready to be thrown open.

Eric replied with a single quick nod, giving him the signal to go.

§§§

CHAPTER TWENTY

MRS. WINTERS BOARDING HOUSE
TULIP, ARKANSAS

The man who called himself Isaac James Taylor watched the last of the elongated convoy of freight wagons pull into a marshaling area on the west side of the sprawling Confederate camp. He was wearing a white starched shirt—the stiff inch-tall collar was unbuttoned and standing open—over a pair of khaki colored canvas pants held up by red fabric braces. A curious look came over his face.

That is odd ... They did not try to unload a single one. Just unhitched the teams and tied them up to the picket line.

He laid the binoculars down on the night stand and picked up the yellow pad of paper.

Suddenly, the bedroom door swung open wide and banged lightly against the side wall. A huge Confederate colonel filled the doorway with menacing blued revolvers in each hand.

The blond haired colonel took three quick steps, closing the distance between them. "Keep your hands where I can see them," he barked.

A major slid in behind him and stepped aside and brought his .44 caliber Colt up level with his icy cold blue eyes.

Taylor's heart skipped a beat. "Easy gents. I am just a travelin' salesman trying to get over a bit of stomach troubles." He forced a wan smile. "Eatin' in different places every week and such."

The young colonel was not buying his act. He holstered the Remington in his left hand without even looking down.

He motioned for the suspected Yankee spy to move away from the window. "One step this way … Put your hands over you head and keep them there." The colonel's voice was not as loud as his first command, but came out lower—like rocks being crushed under a gigantic millstone.

The room was not a huge one. The double bed and nightstand dominated the space, and a small walnut wardrobe served to hold the occupant's clothing. Isaac followed the instructions as he hurriedly contemplated his options.

Diving out the second story window appeared to be only the physically viable means of escape. Isaac's eyes nervously darted from the colonel's grim face to the that of the major. The muzzle of his Colt .44 looked like a huge sewer pipe from only four feet away.

Doran grinned. "I see what you are thinking, mister. Do not even think about divin' out that window behind you. Those wooden mullions are a whole lot tougher than you think … you ain't got a Chinaman's chance without at least a twenty foot head start."

"Not to mention the fact that we would kill you twice before the broken glass and fall did." Eric's eyes narrowed. "What's on the note pad?"

"Oh this? You see, I am just tryin' to pass the time while I am recuperating. I tried to guess how many wagons would be coming in today." He faked a smile. "There sure are a lot of you soldiers."

"Yes, there are," Doran said. He stuck out his left hand. "You wouldn't mind letting us read your little pad, would you?"

"Just a bunch of scribbles of a bored man, I assure ... ."

Doran cut him off. "Hand it over. I will not ask twice." He noted a slight tremor in the hand that held the pad as Isaac released it.

Ingrham took one step back as he rapidly read the last entries. Using the conical brass front sight of his revolver, he flipped the previous page over and read its entries as well.

He turned to Eric. "Got enough to hold him for a military tribunal. Detailed counts of personnel and materiel arriving since yesterday."

"Wait! I can explain," Isaac's voice went up an octave.

"Nose to the wall, mister." Doran's words were as serious as a heart attack. He tossed the note pad on the bed and motioned for him to move to the south wall beside a small window. The major kept him covered. "Spread your feet and do not try anything stupid. This six shooter has a hair trigger."

"You are making a mistake. I am an honest business man," Taylor protested.

Ingrham patted the man down for weapons.

Eric stepped to the nightstand beside the bed. He picked up the binoculars and examined them carefully before tossing them on the bed. "US Army issue field glasses ... Just like the ones that I took off a dead Yankee. Where did you get 'em?"

"I won them in a poker game."

"Where was that?"

"Uh, Little Rock ... No, it was Arkadelphia."

Doran pulled a latigo pigging string out of his tunic. "Keep him covered, Eric ... All right, mister whatever your name is, place your right hand behind your back."

"What are you going to do?" asked Taylor.

Doran slammed the butt of his Colt onto the back of Taylor's skull, staggering him and bloodying his nose against the wall. "I am gonna crush your skull if I have to ask again. Put your right hand behind your back ... Now."

Taylor moaned but did as he was told.

Eric moved to a corner on his left to keep an unencumbered field of fire on the suspected spy.

Doran slipped the loose end of the half inch wide latigo through the prepared loop on the other end and pulled it tight on Taylor's wrist.

He reached up and grabbed the man's left hand and yanked it down forcefully. With skills honed in cattle camp in the Big Bend area as a young man, he crossed the man's wrists, and quickly made a triple wrap that would not let go easily. He tucked the tail of the strap under the last wrap, and pulled it into a single knot.

Ingrham grabbed the man's shoulder and spun him around. A foot long trail of blood had run down the wallpaper and a similar streak stained his once pristine shirt.

"Mister Taylor, if that is your real name, I, Colonel Eric Schmidt, Confederate States of America, hereby charge and arrest you under the Espionage Acts, as provided by our regulations."

"You can not do this. I am a civilian. I am an honest businessman ... I have never been in the army in my life!"

"Save it for the tribunal. They will ascertain your guilt or innocence." Eric picked up the binoculars and yellow pad. He eased back out of the room and kept his handgun at the ready.

"Come on, we have not got all day." Doran pushed the prisoner toward the door.

The officer led him to the stairs, and Eric started down first with Taylor in the middle.

Master Sergeant Wilson turned at the sound of footsteps descending the stairs. Woody could see three sets of legs coming down before he could see a face.

He turned to Eloise. "Looks like they found something."

"What on earth is going on?" she asked.

"Reckon we'll find out in a minute or so," he said with a smile. He noted the familiar face of his regimental commander. The smile vanished quickly when Woody recognized the prisoner. "Son of a bitch."

Woody quickly turned to apologize to Mrs. Winter for his course language in polite company. "Sorry, Ma'am. It just come out, sudden like."

Eric saw Woody's reaction. "You know this yahoo?"

"You bet, Colonel. That there is Jubal Hopkins. Backsliding sumbuck if ever there was one. He was in my company down in San Antone."

Woody's disgust for the man was obvious. "He's one of the few that went back north when the US Army surrendered the fort to Texas after we seceded from the Union."

"Damned lie. I never saw that man before. My name is Isaac Taylor. I told you, ask Mrs. Winters." The bloodied man was defiant.

Woody's ire was raised. "Call me a liar will you? Colonel, Jubal has an eagle tattoo on his left breast." He pointed at his own chest. "Right here."

"That man is insane! Do not pay him any heed!" The spy was starting to sweat profusely.

Eric smiled and he reached for the knife on his belt. Slipping it out, he offered it butt first to the maters sergeant. "Show me the ink, but do not mess up Mrs. Winters' parlor. Got it?"

"You betcha, Colonel … Nary a drop. I promise." Woody took the razor sharp blade and snipped off the top five buttons on Jubal's shirt. He wiped off the blood stains from Hopkin's nose bleed onto the shaking man's shoulder and handed the cleaned blade back to Eric.

Williams leaned in close to the spy's right ear. "Bet you never thought that we would cross paths again, did ya?" He placed the fingers of both hands inside the man's cotton undergarment and ripped it wide open down to the naval. He pulled back the left side—exposing a stylized eagle with his head turned sideways.

"See for yourself, Colonel. My eyes play no tricks on me. Just like I remembered."

"You go straight to hell, Woody." Jubal spat in his face.

Woody unloaded a right cross than sent the spy reeling to the floor.

Eloise gasped and sprang to her feet, covering her mouth. "Is he a Yankee … a filthy Yankee spy?" Something about the way she said *Yankee* dripped with venom.

Doran dragged Jubal to his feet.

Eric nodded. "Appears so, Ma'am. He lied to us about serving in the army. Lied about his name."

He held up the captured binoculars. "Likely lied about winning these in a poker game up in Little Rock."

She appeared to suddenly fall almost ill. "And to think I was fixin' his supper." Eloise drifted out of the room in a daze, her shoulders slumped and dispirited.

Doran let go of Jubal. "Colonel, think we need to go over his room with a fine tooth comb?"

"Perhaps. Think we already have enough proof to get a conviction in a military tribunal."

"I demand to see a lawyer. I am a soldier in the United States Army," Jubal blurted.

"Demand all you want, Mister Hopkins. We caught you red handed in the act of committing espionage. Spying while not in uniform is punishable by firing squad. You should know that."

The spy started to reply when the room was shook by the thunderous crack of a Colt .44 . He hunched over, looking down briefly at the exit wound over his heart. His legs became rubber and buckled. Jubal toppled over face down in the entryway.

Eric's hand flew to his revolver as he spun to face the direction the shot came from. He watched as a smoking gun fell from the grip of the grief-stricken widow woman.

She sank to her knees and brought her hands together in front as she bowed her head. "Lord take me now for I have sinned. I could not possibly live with a murderin' Yankee in my home."

Doran was closest to her. He kicked the gun out of arm's reach and helped her to her feet. "Come, Eloise, let us sit you down." He led her to the same Chippendale couch as before.

She collapsed onto it, and Doran knelt beside her holding her hand.

Woody Williams stared at the body of the spy. Warm crimson colored blood was still oozing from the bullet wound on his back. "What we gonna do now, Colonel? What about her?" He tilted he head toward Eloise.

Eric pointed at the dead man and motioned toward the front door. "Drag his useless carcass out of here. We shall clean up the mess as best we can. God's will has been done, as far as I am concerned."

"If you are happy, color me thrilled." He shook his head. "Never liked that man … Never did."

Eric nodded. "Woody, you are a great judge of character." He grinned for a second then the seriousness of the entire business that had just transpired took over.

"Excellent catch on the binoculars, Master Sergeant. You might have made the difference in the success of this whole operation."

"You flatter me, sir. I am just a horse soldier doin' his duty."

"Bull feathers", Doran said as he got to his feet. "I am thinkin' you might have saved three to four hundred lives … maybe ours."

"Major Ingrham is right. I will be putting you in for a commendation and another stripe," Eric said.

Woody chuckled. He reached down and grabbed the dead man's wrists—still bound by the leather strap. "You know, Jubal … I might have been wrong about you. Maybe you were good for something after all."

Doran stepped over and grabbed the man's boots. "Do not get yourself in a rush and cut that latigo off when we get him outside. Might want to use it again."

Eric held the door open as the other men carried the body outside. He glanced back at the widow as tears rolled down her face.

§§§

CHAPTER TWENTY-ONE

ARKANSAS RIVER FERRY CROSSING

Bass Reeves looked nervously at the ramp leading up to the ferry. He never had learned to swim and the thought of him falling into the deep waters of the slow moving Arkansas River bothered him to no end.

The chain driven ferry chugged to a slow halt on the southwest side. A cavalryman from the Texas Second Regiment served as new ferry master. He dropped the gate and with the help of another trooper, and called out in a loud voice, "Walk your mounts all the way to the far end, boys. Pack 'em in tight and try to keep 'em calm. We ain't got all day."

Bass noted one rider had taken the trip back from the far side. He waved at a familiar face as the lead elements of his master's company began the loading process. "Howdy, Major Ingrham. I done that new trot you called posting … jest like you showed me. My backside, it wants me to say thank you." He grinned broadly.

Doran laughed. "Told you it would help."

Bass noticed a wide smear of dried blood on the major's uniform. His smile immediately faded into a look of concern.

"Mister Major, did you go an' gets yourself hurt?" He pointed at the older man's arm.

Doran glanced down and grinned, his blue eyes sparkling. "Thanks for asking, but praise the Lord, it ain't mine … least not this time. A dozen Yankees were left guarding this river crossing. I took thirty of my company for a little swim a few miles downstream." He pointed toward an area with small rolling hills. "Never saw us coming from the east."

Bass nodded. "Y'all been here a while, I s'pose?"

"'Bout two hours, I figure. We left camp just before sunrise." Ingrham brought his mount up to a lope and headed toward the rear of the column.

It came Bass' turn to walk Whiskey onto the wooden barge. There was a heavy rail fence on both sides, but the ends were made of straight grain pine resembling picket fence slats with ropes woven around and connecting each one to the next.

The top rope could be detached from one end and the fencing laid off to the side until the cargo was moved safely on onboard .

He held his mount's lead rope up close and whispered to him, "We gets to take us a short boat ride, Whiskey. That way neither one of us gets wet. What do you think of that?"

The horse did not seem to mind the bustle and congestion as much as the rider. It followed the horses ahead of it, and they all crowded in together as the ferry master, and his assistant re-hung the rear gate.

A slight hiss of steam signaled the start of the return voyage. The driver had already reversed the gear direction of the chain capstan. When steam pressure was sent to the piston, a long arm connected to a geared pulley drove a separate beveled gear mated to the capstan.

Bass was standing close enough to see the heavy two inch chain being fed into the simple but ingenious device. He looked forward to see wet chain being lifted out of the river, run alongside the boat in cast iron rings and through the drive mechanism.

Don't that beat all? Looks a little like what they use on a train ... but all through that itty bitty contraption. If'n they did the same thing on them wagons, we wouldn't be needin' all these hayburners.

He patted Whiskey on the side of his neck and chuckled at his whimsical thoughts of future self-propelled vehicles.

Doran approached the first one of his sergeants providing perimeter security a half mile out on the convoy flanks. "How goes it, Jim Bob?"

"Nary a soul moving from the south. Been Wearing these new glasses out." He let the binoculars hang from a strap around his neck. "How much time you reckon we got until them Yankees in Pine Bluff know we are on the move?"

Ingrham laughed. "If I was that smart they'd make me a General ... Would lay even money that they knew we arrived in Tulip. Two to one, they did not know we pulled out at dawn." He stifled a yawn.

"Think we will get the three regiments across the river today?"

"That is our plan. The new units are not used to pushing like Colonel Schmidt wants 'em to ... The main thing is, we do not want to get into an extended engagement with the Yanks."

"Any way you look at it, it was dang sure a good thing that Woody had his eyes peeled. Hard as hell to hide close to a thousand men and their gear in a town the size of Tulip."

Doran nodded. "Wasn't any secret, but we sure didn't need a damn Yankee spy peeing in our mess kit. I pity the poor little widow woman that has to live with her guilt of shootin' the weasel bastard."

"Would you have shot him yourself after the tribunal?"

"In the blink of an eye. But it is strictly business with me." Doran cleared his throat. "You hardly ever see me killing somebody, just 'cause they pissed me off ... any more."

Jim Bob gave a high pitched nervous laugh. "You be funnin' me ... right, Major?"

Doran crossed his gloved hands on the pommel of his saddle. He leaned closer to the twenty-four year old from Fort Worth. His blue eyes narrowed to little more than slits as he stared at him.

Ingram did not even blink. "Am I?"

The sergeant felt the hairs stand up on the back of his neck. His throat suddenly became dry as a Sonoran desert dust devil.

Doran wheeled his pony and headed for the next sentry post.

The ferry bumped into the landing pier on the northeast side of the river with a noticeable jolt. Bass turned to glance at the ferry driver, who merely shrugged, and then closed off the steam valve to the single drive piston.

The operator and his assistant pulled the front barrier to the side as the first five riders walked their mounts up the plank incline and onto the dry dirt roadway.

"Keep moving until everybody is off the ferry," Captain George Reeves called out as he looked back over his shoulder.

One by one, each man tightened his girth and remounted.

George looked back across the river to see at least a dozen more men from his company awaiting passage. The ferry had already departed for the opposite side. He made a command decision and passed it to his first sergeant. "I want to assemble up on that first ridge up there. As soon as the last man is across, we will depart en masse."

"Yes, sir." He reined halfway around to face the majority of the men. "Second Company ... Column of threes ... forward at a walk ... Ho!"

Bass fell into the group near the middle. His eyes caught sight of a flight of buzzards circling a spot a few hundred yards from the river. *Wonder what they be seein'?*

When the company reached the crest of the ridge, his curiosity ended abruptly. Twelve bodies, stripped of all their uniforms and gear lay stacked like so much cordwood. Their off white undergarments were stained with blood.

Bass saw several with gaping head wounds. Swarms of black and green flies buzzed incessantly.

Their uniforms were folded neatly beside the roadway, and their weapons were stashed beside them, awaiting a passing wagon with space available.

"Lawd o' mercy", Bass whispered. He suddenly remembered his brief conversation with Major Ingram. *Never saw us coming from the east.*

For Bass, the true meaning of the *horrors of war* became real for the first time in his life.

§§§

CHAPTER TWENTY-TWO

BANKS OF THE MISSISSIPPI

Colonel Hebert handed the binoculars to Eric. "See that black dot on the other side?"

"The one to left of the dead cypress with the eagle nest up about two thirds to the top?"

"Right. That is the remains of the main house. There used to be a dock to the south of it, but I cannot spot it from here."

"Is that where we will be aiming for on the east bank?" Eric stared at the churning swirls of muddy water—the color of strong coffee with cream. This was the first time he had actually laid eyes on the storied river that challenged them to cross.

"I hope so. We will put together some skiffs from the smaller planks. It will take at least two full days to cut and assemble the barge, I think." Hebert turned back toward the horses. "If the topographic charts are correct, there should be a oxbow about fifty yards south of here."

"You cannot even see fifty yards in this underbrush."

"Not until after the big floods ... Then all this undergrowth gets a free one-way trip to the Gulf. That is also when the river picks itself a new channel and leaves us these crescent shaped oxbows."

Andre led the way, pushing his way through small cedars and ten foot tall dogwoods.

Eric unsheathed his saber to slice through green briars that seemed to snagged his tunic at every opportunity.

"Ah ha," Andre called out. "We found it."

"Found it? I am still hung up in these blasted thorns." Eric's voice conveyed his frustration. After a few yards, he stood beside the Cajun gazing at a crystal blue expanse of water that grew to 800 yards wide and extended for almost three miles, although neither man could see more than three quarters of a mile as it curved gracefully to the west and then back to the south and east.

"This is what you call an oxbow?" Eric asked.

"It is, my friend, and this is where we will build and launch the ferry. Ships passing by on the river cannot see this because of all the trees that have grown up in the hundreds of years since this channel was abandoned."

"This water is unbelievably clear. Hard to believe it was once part of the Big Muddy."

Andre smiled. "If I am right, it is still teaming with catfish and bass. The men we do not need for clearing trees, digging a connecting channel or actually involved in constructing the barge and launch ramp can be put to work fishing."

"I see what you meant about the availability of timber. There are thousands of virgin pines and cypress lining the shore." He gazed up at the tree tops—Some were over one hundred feet high. "Reminds me of the deep piney woods back home. These cypress trees look like those did around Caddo lake."

Andre nodded. "I looked at these river banks every day for years, but only stopped where we had docks to drop off or pick up goods and passengers. It looks much different to be inside these woods for a change."

"I imagine it does." Eric swatted a mosquito that had begun to feed on his neck. "Expect we should get back to the column and see where the sawmill is. We will want to get it set up as close to the launch site as practical, don't you think?"

"Let us talk to the men with boat building and logging experience first. No sense in making their job harder than necessary."

Bass's torso glistened like a Greek statue carved from black granite. The heat of the late July summer was stifling, and he had shed his long sleeved shirt as well as his hat. Sunlight almost never reached the ground due to the thick canopy high above him.

Bass leaned into the two-man saw—sometimes called a misery whip—as his partner tugged on the other end. Each stroke of the newly purchased tool took another half inch cut out of the four foot diameter loblolly pine that towered over them.

"Hold on a second," Bass said. The muscular black man wiped the sweat off his brow and dabbed the burning salty drops away that were stinging his eyes. "Ain't got us a lick of breeze down in these woods, is we?"

"Naw, not today." His coworker, Chuck Norris, an experienced lumberjack before the war started, gauged the depth of the first cut. "We best pull out and get the wedges driven in before it closes down on us and locks the blade tight as a tick."

The two backed the seven foot saw out and set it aside. Chuck grabbed a narrow steel wedge and drove it four inches into the saw cut, using a square headed machinist hammer. He repeated the process again about every foot around the circumference of the fresh saw kerf.

"That should hold it until we get the break angle cut. Can you hand me that?" Chuck pointed at a double bladed ax he had spent hours the previous night sharpening—first using a fine tooth mill bastard file and finishing up with a hard Arkansas stone.

Not as tall as Bass Reeves, Chuck barely topped six feet. However he more than made up for inches with pounds of muscle packed on his arms, shoulders, and chest.

"All right, now. Stand back … Let us see if I did a good job on this new chopper." Chuck steadied his feet into the dense pine needle litter which blanketed the ground around the ill-fated loblolly.

He took in a deep breath, let it out, and grasped the hickory handle as if he were ready to swing a baseball bat. The sandy haired man from Tyler, Texas, took a quick look at where he wanted the tree to fall. He adjusted his stance a few inches to the left and brought the ax head high over his right shoulder.

Bass watched in amazement at the speed at which the man brought the blade into contact with the thick pine bark. The steel sank a full two inches on the first blow.

Chuck repeated the downward blow and then made two aggressive hits—slightly lower with a with a shallow upward angle. A chuck of wood and bark almost the size of a loaf of bread popped off the trunk.

"Whoo whee! I ain't never seed a white boy work like that." Bass was grinning from ear to ear.

"Hit it like you live, my daddy always says." Chuck continued for a couple of minutes until he had a large V notch cut out—eighteen inches high and perhaps twenty inches deep. He laid the ax down.

"Come on. Grab that bucksaw, and we will be laying this big son of a gun right between those two little ones." Chuck pointed toward the sandy road coursing through the forest.

"You sound like you know what you be doin'. Me … I jest keep my eyes open and my mouth shut." Bass leaned over and grabbed on to the saw's handle.

Chuck showed him where to start the final cut. In a few short minutes, the saw was almost halfway through the trunk. He felt the slightest binding as the massive tree began to settle on the blade.

"Hold on. Let me wedge it, and we can finish," he said.

With much curiosity, Bass watched as Chuck drove two more steel triangles deep in the kerf. He dropped the hammer and took hold of the saw once again. "Two more inches, Bass, and we will be ready to drop this mongoose."

Bass nodded and gave the saw all he was worth —even as he wondered what a mongoose was. He looked at the two kerfs that almost touched in the middle. "How we gonna get this saw outta the tree with them metal thangs jammed in there?

"No problem, my friend. When the trunk snaps off, the momentum will carry it past the stump. The weight will be off those little boogers, and we can just pick 'em up."

"I trust you be knowing what we do."

"Go make sure nobody is coming up the trail. Once it starts down, I cain't stop it."

Bass nodded and jogged thirty yards to the roadway. He could hear other teams sawing in the woods, but the road itself was clear. He jogged back. "The trail be clear."

Chuck took the hammer and pounded one wedge in flush. The tree made a definite cracking sound.

Bass' eye's grew wide, but Norris only grinned as he simply said, "Not yet." He skipped a wedge and drove the next one flush. The tree cracked ominously and much louder than before.

Bass kept his eyes on his partner. The white logger was not nervous. Bass swallowed at a lump that was beginning to form in his throat.

Chuck moved to the middle wedge and prepared to hit it. He glanced at Bass. "Forgot to tell you … Never take your eyes off the tree. Do not turn you back on it. If it starts to fall wrong and look like it is gonna crush you like a June bug, step to the side … left or right, I do not care which way."

Bass nodded vigorously.

"If you try to run away, these big boys will fall faster than you can run. Understand what I am sayin'?"

"Yassah."

"Good. That about covers it … I forgot. You wanna yell *Timberrrrr*?"

"Timber?"

"Yep, but loud and long. Lets the other lumberjacks know one's a comin' down."

"I can do that."

Chuck gave him a strange look and shrugged.

"Oh, you mean right now," Bass said, slightly embarrassed

"Sometime today." Chuck snickered.

Bass inhaled deeply and bellowed out a deep yell, "TIMBERRRRR!"

Chuck drove the critical wedge into the kerf and jumped back a few feet. Slowly, at first, the loblolly pine began to lean, and a brief series of cracking turned into a single pop loud as a pistol shot. With ever increasing speed, the 115 foot tall denizen of the forest tilted over, crashed to the ground, and bounced once before coming to rest.

Bass was surprised by the speed and violence of the toppling. He let out a low whistle.

Chuck stuck out his hand. "Now you can tell your grandkids about the day you became a bona fide lumberjack."

Bass eagerly took his hand and grinned.

§§§

CHAPTER TWENTY-THREE

NORTHEAST ARKANSAS
CONFEDERATE CAMP

Colonel Schmidt rode his black stallion up to the portable lumber mill. His team had lashed together temporary tripods topped with long peeled pine poles rigged up to utilize the power of leverage to lift the uncut logs felled by the multiple teams of lumberjacks.

Crews of soldiers carried off the larger piles of waste to make way for the two inch thick planks that were being cut for the barge exterior and deck. Sets of steel rollers—mounted to what appeared to be essentially heavy saw horses with adjustable steel rollers—supported the weight of the logs as they were fed to the six foot diameter ripping blade.

He watched for a minute as the rapidly spinning blade inched its way through the raw wood, creating a continuous cascade of yellow sawdust under the machine.

After the log passed the cutting edge, three men took hold of the finished plank, and the operator changed the movable fence, allowing two others to push the log back on the far side and get ready for the feed crew to run it through again.

The sawmill blade itself might have been steam powered, but there was plenty of hard manual labor involved in its operation.

Eric looked on as a soldier driving a team of horses dragging a thirty foot log brought in the next one to be processed. *It is remarkable how straight these loblolly pines grow here. Not much waste in these specimens.*

He could hear the sound of a dozen men chopping the branches from the upper growth of the downed trees. He turned and cleared the area to his left, and then reined Thunder around and trotted down the newly made road to the barge construction site.

Eric ground tied his mount between two towering pines. Looking around, he spotted the affable Cajun supervising the construction of the barge.

Andre stepped out from under the first six hull planks laid down on the raised framework built to support the weight of the finished structure. He had stripped off his woolen Confederate officer tunic and was wearing his long-sleeved undergarment. It showed several black splotches where he had come into contact with the tar being used to seal the joints.

"Eric, my friend. Care to join us?" He grinned broadly.

"Thank you kind sir, but I must demure." Eric laughed. "Believe I am a little too tall to fit under the south side." He pointed at the far end of the frame.

The massive support structure resembled a pier and beam house with huge floor joists running the width of the planned ferry.

It was only three feet above the ground while the near supports were seven feet high, some sixty feet farther from the water's edge.

He took off his riding gloves, tucked them neatly under his gun belt, and folded them over to keep them in place as he walked around the perimeter.

A long freight wagon carrying eight more of the three inch thick planks—each measuring over thirty feet in length—pulled up beside the job site. The wagon bed was a full twenty feet long with the last ten feet of the fresh cut lumber hanging past the tail gate.

Andre dusted off his hands as he approached Eric. "I do not hold that against you … not for a minute," Andre replied with a grin. "I must say, it is easier to pilot one than build one."

"Think it will hold water?"

Andre nodded as he pointed to a crew of eight working steadily with hand planes. "Those men are putting an inch and a half rabbet cut in each plank. It makes a much stronger joint than a butt joint."

"I see that. Is that also known as ship lap?"

The Cajun nodded. "The overlapping seams cut leaks to a minimum. Works in exterior walls as well. We are packing the joints with oakum and tar."

"I understand now why you wanted the planks as wide as possible. That hand work with planes must be the overall limiting factor in the speed of construction."

"Quite possibly. When we get to the interior frame work, the four by six stringers require bore holes and pilot holes for the lag screws ... And that will mean a lot of holes drilled."

"We brought a dozen braces and bits. Two men per drill should keep the men from wearing themselves out in an hour." Eric gazed down at the half dozen smaller pine trees peeled of their bark. Workers had laid them out parallel to each other—forming a ramp between the building frame and the water.

He pointed at the poles. "Will we be covering them with lard when the time comes to launch?"

"Yes, indeed. Did not want to attract critters before then. By the way, how is the digging going on the canal?"

"Funny you should ask. We have sixty men working with shovels and another ten with pick axes and saws … Just to take out the tree roots. Some of those are booger bears. They are taking it down to just above the water level now."

"How are they disposing of the dug out soil? Did the river work well as a dispensing agent?"

Eric grinned. "You know it. The river is already so full of dirt, another acre or so will not be noticed. We have another ten men making trip after trip with wheelbarrows."

"Think they can get it done in two days?"

"If they put their backs into it. The dirt is not that hard to dig in. Mostly sand and tree litter. It will get nasty when it gets wet, though … might have to switch to buckets if it gets too soupy for shovels."

A Union gun boat appeared as it churned its way upstream from Vicksburg headed to Saint Louis. One of four lookouts stationed near the Confederate crossing spot lowered his field glasses, whistled to another soldier, and pointed as the sternwheeler rounded the bend to the south.

His compatriot motioned to a third man who promptly snugged the girth on his horse and swung aboard. In a second, he disappeared into the towering vegetation lining the Mississippi.

"Yankee boat's on the river," he called as he slowed down only long enough to warn the supervisor of the canal dig.

The master sergeant nodded and relayed the message as he walked along the seventy foot wide ditch. He made a hand signal placing a single finger over his lips as the sweating men passed the critical message on to the next closest worker.

Riding to the sawmill, Corporal Jenkins passed the word before heading to the barge build site. He spotted Colonel Schmidt and reined up beside him. "Sir, another Yankee gun boat headed north."

"Armored or not?" the commander replied.

"Just a sternwheeler with a front deck gun. Might have one of those rifled breach loaders in the back as well, but it was too far away to tell, sir."

"Good work, Jenkins. Let the lumberjacks know. Give 'em a twenty minute break to let it pass out of earshot."

"Will do, Colonel." He reined back and turned the dappled gray Appaloosa around and trotted back up to the main roadway the force had made though the forest.

Bass Reeves looked up and saw the young corporal pass nearby and call out, "Yankees on the river. Take twenty minutes." He rode on to keep passing the message to the other work crews.

"'Bout time we take another breather," Chuck said as he wiped the sweat from his forehead. "What time you figger it is?"

"Hard to say," Bass replied as he looked up into the dense forest canopy. "Must be 'round three or so. Been a while since we ate them sammiches for lunch."

"I 'spect that is right." Chuck drained the last of his water from his canteen. "If that don't beat all." He screwed the cap back on in disgust.

Bass handed him his own canteen. "Gots some left. It be your if you want it."

"Do not mind if I do." Norris drained the last of Bass's canteen. "What say we mosey on down the to the lake? I heard them say it is purty and blue as the sky."

"I am game. Better hang my shirt up here where we can find this tree. All theses here woods ... To me it looks just alike."

Chuck grinned. "Heard that before, I have."

Doran shook his head at the recruit. "No, son. If you want the horse to lay down for you, first thing you gotta do is get control of its head. Watch again." He reached under the pony's neck and grabbed the chain under the bridle. He held horse's head down and, using his boot, tapped its left fore leg lightly.

The horse responded by lifting its left foot to the rear.

"Continue to apply down pressure on the bridle while you touch the right leg." He repeated again gently tapping the other leg.

The horse complied by pulling its right leg back and kneeling.

Doran poked a finger into the base of the horse's neck. As he pulled lightly on the horse's head, he spoke softly to it, "Down."

He stepped back to keep his legs clear.

The horse rolled over on its left side.

"See how I told you to keep the pony off of your legs? They will hurt you if you are not careful." He patted the horse on the neck to calm it. "Good boy. That was not too bad, was it?" He stroked the horse's neck several times.

"You want the horse to not be afraid of lying down. Their natural instinct is to stand. They are vulnerable when they lie down. Understand?"

"Think I got it, Major. You make it look easy."

"It is easy, if you know how horses think. After a couple weeks, you can just poke them in the side on the neck and say, 'Down'." He grinned. "Someday, I might write a book about it."

"Bet it would be a good one. Whatcha gonna call it?"

Doran mulled the question over for a moment. "Hell. Keep it simple. How about *Think Like a Horse*?"

"Sound kinda silly. Do horses think?"

The silver haired cowboy shook his head. "More than some people I know."

§§§

CHAPTER TWENTY-FOUR

ARKANSAS RIVER CROSSING

The Union cavalry replacement detail approached the ferry crossing warily. The senior enlisted man stopped a quarter mile from the river and scanned the area with his binoculars. He could see the ferry was docked on the far side and a figure in blue was seated under a shade tree nearby.

Seven pup tents were still in place as had been the custom since the rebels had raided the railroad shipment several weeks previously. The lone man stood up and waved at the group of riders and another left the cover of a tent, walked to another one and went inside.

"Rather strange," the sergeant remarked. I can see seven horses on a picket line ... but only two people."

The man under the tree moved down to the barge and stuck a few sticks of kindling into the firebox. The coals ignited the dry sapwood, and it gave off a wispy column of gray smoke as the man on the ferry waved again at the stationary military detail.

A corporal looked in all directions. No other riders were in sight. "Sergeant, maybe they are all sleeping. Could have stayed up all night playing cards or somethin'."

"Or somethin'", the senior man groused. "Most likely tippin' a bottle of Old Crow ... I will have their drunk asses in a sling." He bumped his spurs into the brown gelding's flanks.

The others followed along behind him.

The soldier serving as the ferry operator slipped a larger piece of firewood into the firebox. He closed off the relief valve on the boiler and watched the needle climb on the pressure gauge up to 200 PSI. A slight smile came to his lips. He glanced up at the approaching riders. They had closed to three hundred yards. He moved the capstan shift lever into gear, and the empty ferry lurched into motion.

The relief NCO reined up at the edge of the ferry dock. He was indeed displeased at the appearance of the man running the ferry. One side of his uniform shirt was untucked, and his pants were drooped outside his boots. The man has his head hung low, his cavalry hat covering his face. He was leaning onto his long gun like it was a crutch.

The sergeant could not see the man's face, but the uniform and body size had to be Corporal Smithers.

"Smitty! Where the hell is everyone? And what is wrong with you? Have you been drinking?"

The ferry driver bent over and made an awful noise. What looked like vomit splattered onto the ferry deck. "Sick ... Musta been bad chow last night."

"Oh for Pete's sake ... Man, have you no pride?" The sergeant was clearly not amused.

The blued steel muzzle of a .58 caliber Enfield slipped out between two tent flaps on the opposite bank of the Arkansas. The color case hardened hammer made two distinct clicks as the unseen shooter drew it back to full cock.

As the ferry approached twenty yards from the southwest bank, the operator turned to look toward the steam tank. He lifted his left hand as if to point at the pressure gage.

When his hand dropped, a thunderous volley of rifle fire erupted from inside the tents on the far side of the river. Four of the seven Union soldiers tumbled out of their saddles. The NCO was drawing his sidearm when the deathly ill ferry operator miraculously recovered, sprang into life, and leveled a double barreled shotgun at him.

The blast of 00 buckshot caught the sergeant high in the chest. A look of shock and disbelief was etched on his face as the last thought to ever cross his mind flashed into his consciousness before fading to black. *You are not Smitty!*

His body flopped back onto the high cantle, sliding out of the saddle as his sorrel horse turned and bolted away.

Two surviving soldiers wheeled around to escape the bloody ambush. A Confederate corporal threw back a tan canvas tarp covering his hideout beside the steam engine's wood pile. As he was taking a quick kneeling position, Master Sergeant Woody Williams thumbed back the hammer on the left barrel and fired again. One of the two riders slumped forward and rolled off into the dry brown grass.

A single rifle shot from the corporal found its mark. Three riderless startled horses galloped southeastward in the direction from which they had come, loose reins dragging along beneath them.

"Damnation, Woody. Yer plan worked slicker'n snot on a doorknob," exclaimed the corporal.

"Yep. Reckon it did at that." He reached over to take the capstan drive into neutral as the ferry approached the landing. He looked off in the distance to see four riders leaving concealment in the woods a full half mile from the ferry.

"They should have no problem cuttin' off them Yankee horses. Might buy us and the boys at the Big Muddy 'nother day or two."

The corporal nodded. "'Spect we best make sure them bluebellies is all dead." He drew his Colt revolver and pointed to the closest bodies.

Williams unshaven face was grim. "Strip 'em as usual. Stow their gear, and we will bury 'em in the river, just like the last ones. Picket their horses on the other side of the ridge." He spat out a chew of tobacco and watched it float down the river for a moment.

Bass Reeve filled his canteen a second time. The lake water tasted good, and the July heat kept him and the other woodsmen drenched in sweat. "Sho is purty over here. Don't know of a lake like this un back where I comes from."

"We got a few in east Texas. Seen Caddo Lake a time or two. Big enough for a man to get hisself lost on, that one is, " Chuck said between drinks from his canteen.

"Do tell?" Bass swatted a mosquito, leaving bloody smear on his belly. "They got bugs like this over there?"

"Big enough to carry off women and children."

Bass grinned. "You know, the preacher ... he say a man goes to hell for lyin'."

Chuck nodded and smiled.

§§§

CHAPTER TWENTY-FIVE

NORTHEAST ARKANSAS
CONFEDERATE CAMP

It was late on the second day when the last of the top deck was screwed to the framework underneath. Eric heard a sharp crack of thunder and stared up at the towering thunderstorm building south of the camp.

He moved closer to Andre. "Did you see the Cumulonimbus?"

Andre gave him a questioning look. "The what?"

Eric grinned. "Sorry ... Blame that on my mother's Latin books. Heaped rain cloud in English." He pointed south.

Andre frowned. "That is not good, my friend. Open water is no place to be in a bad storm. Particularly when your head is the highest thing on the boat." He turned back to Eric. "Have you been watching it long?"

He nodded. "First spotted it around thirty minutes ago. It is a lot bigger now ... Think it is moving east." He tilted his head toward the distant riverbank.

"We should have the steam engine and drive gear mounted and bolted down in half an hour. The gin poles, A frame and pulleys are all in place for the lift and transfer."

"And the rowboats are all assembled and ready?" Eric asked.

"Just waiting on your signal to proceed. One has six hundred feet of rope on board, and we will have another twenty four hundred feet coiled up on this side."

Colonel Schmidt mulled over the plan. "What if we stationed two of the skiffs, each about a third of the way across the river. If we then suspended the rope's weight ... or at least part of it ... would that help us to pull the mass of the rope through the water? We will not have any horses on the other side."

Andre closed his eyes and envisioned Eric's idea. He opened his eyes and smiled. "Excellent idea, my friend. That plan could aid us particularly when we get into pulling the chain across." He called out to a workman. "Stephen, do we have enough lumber for a forth or fifth rowboat?"

"No problem, Colonel. We will have to fashion some more oars, though."

"Let the others finish installing the fences on the barge. Make us two more skiffs."

The man waved at a couple of other carpenters and motioned for them to join him. The three men headed for a stack of surplus planks and cutoff pieces left near the main road.

Another bolt of lighting struck the ground a mile or so south of the camp—five seconds later, the crash of thunder boomed. Eric studied the boiling tops of the cloud for a few seconds. For some odd reason, the formation reminded him of popped corn.

"I will ride back to the closest clearing where I can see the weather to the west. Keep the work going, and we can make a decision when I return."

He strode quickly to his black stallion, grabbed the reins and took to the saddle.

The sky was much more menacing to the south. Eric watched the continuous line of thunderstorms for a couple of minutes. *Not coming this way.* A few other scattered cumulous clouds were starting to block the setting sun. The darker color in the smaller ones meant only one thing to him—*rain is on the way.*

He nudged Thunder into a right turn and checked out the sky to the northwest. A massive thunderstorm—one that dwarfed the one closest to the camp—was pushing up past 70,000 feet into the atmosphere. It was easily over twenty miles across but some sixty miles away.

Colonel Schmidt watched as lightning flashed from cloud to cloud inside the behemoth. He counted silently to himself to time the distance to the sound of thunder that never came. *Thank God, it is much farther away than it looks.*

He kept his eyes on a single part of the storm cell and tracked its movement relative to the tops of pine trees. Judging from the angle that it was north of the setting sun, he came up with a final answer. *It is goin' east. Should miss us by ten miles or more.*

"Come on, big boy. Got things to do." He tapped his heels against the stallion's flanks.

The last section of protective fence rail was up as Eric rode back to the build site. He swung down and dropped the reins.

Andre approached him with a concerned look. "What do you think?"

"My considered opinion is that the heavy storms will pass upriver and down river of us. We might get some rain in the middle of the night, but it is impossible to guess how much … or exactly when for than matter."

He attempted a smile, but it was obvious that the consequences of the decision were weighing on him.

Lieutenant Colonel Hebert nodded. "I truly understand. We must go with the best information available at the time of the decision." He smiled. "Life can be lonely at the top, do you agree?"

"That it is," Eric chuckled. He shot a side glance at the barge. "Still think you can make the Ark float?"

"Certainly hope so. It is far too tilted as it sits to be very useful as a dance floor." Andre winked at his little joke. He motioned Eric to follow him. "Stand over here if you would, sir. When we get it moving, you would not like to be in its path."

"You, sir, are the boat expert ... I am merely an interested observer."

A sizable crowd of lumberjacks, carpenters, and wood workers gathered round as the thick lines were attached to heavy cast iron cleats bolted to the deck.

"Stand clear of the water side. Once she starts, there is no stopping her." Andre called out and motioned for everyone to move back. A lanky young carpenter using a wide hog's hair paint brush slathered semisolid lard from a wooden pail onto the stripped pine poles running parallel all the way to the water.

When he was through, the man stepped to the side and gave him a thumbs up signal.

Andre checked to make sure that the two inch thick lines connected to the deck cleats were properly coiled and the tails tied off to stout trees.

He called out in a load voice, "I need two strong ax men to chop these braces." He pointed at a pair of pine tree logs, each around a foot in diameter and six feet long. Both were wedged into position on the lake side of the platform and already under considerable compression.

Chuck looked at Bass Reeves. "What do you say? I am game if you are."

Bass nodded. "Sounds a little dangerous, but I wants to see this big ol' thing flop into the lake."

Chuck held up his hand. "Got two volunteers here. Need one more ax." He looked around.

Another lumber jack proffered his. Bass took it, and both men walked over to Andre.

The Cajun beamed. "Outstanding. Now what I want you to do is cut the blocking braces right in the middle. The barge will clear the stubs."

Chuck and Bass nodded in unison.

"The tricky part is to cut them both at the same time. I do not want one end to release and the other to stay in place. Do you understand?"

"Yessir," Chuck said.

Bass nodded vigorously. "Yassah. Me and him, we been working together for two days straight. We can do it."

Andre placed his hands on a shoulder of each man. He bowed his head. "Lord, protect these brave men as we launch this vessel. Guide us and direct us to success. All the glory we give to you. In the name of Jesus Christ , our Savior, Amen."

A ripple of *Amens* came from the assembled soldiers.

"Once it starts to move, gentlemen, jump back like your life depends on it ... because it does." Andre's face was deadly serious.

Bass felt his pulse begin to quicken.

Chuck took the nearest brace.

Andre walked with Bass to the far one and pointed at the mid point. "Right about here, I believe."

With the clouds and forest tops blocking the setting sun's rays, the light was beginning to fade early. Bass spread his feet shoulder width apart and looked over as Chuck brought his hands together near the base of the ax handle.

"Together now," Chuck called as he raised the head over his shoulder and back for a full swing.

Bass followed his lead, and the two men brought their blades down in unison. Both blades buried deeply into the trunks.

Each man pried the ax head free and picked out a different spot corresponding to the diameter of the brace for his next blow.

The crowd held its breath as the two men rained down mighty blows in unison. Chunks of wood exploded from the logs.

Chuck glanced over at Bass and gauged the depth of his notch. He smiled. *That boy is a quick learner.*

He brought his ax high once more. Bass mirrored his every move.

The sounds of a dozen bullfrogs croaking floated over the oxbow lake as a squadron of fireflies danced in the gloaming dusk.

Eric checked his gold pocket watch. *Five minutes after seven. If we hurry, we should be able to start the first load by nine.* He returned his gaze to the big black man who was three quarters of the way through the pine log brace. *Will not be long now.*

Chuck held up a single hand, signaling Bass to stop cutting. He tapped the ax blade gently on the remaining wedge of wood in the bottom of the notch and listened to the sound. He could see the pole flex slightly and thought that he heard a groan from the barge.

"She's ready to bust loose," he called to Bass. "Give me one more hard hit … smack dab in the middle. Be ready to jump!"

Bass hollered back. "You got it." He took in a deep breath and brought the ax to his shoulder. Watching Chuck for his timing, he brought his hands up to full extension and gave it all he had.

The two braces shattered with a report like a pistol shot. The upper sections flew free, rotating end over end and landing in the water as the barge started to move.

The squeal of tortured timber on timber drifted out from under the monstrous barge as it accelerated and slid sideways into the placid unsuspecting lake.

Bass was shocked at the size of the splash. A wall of water one hundred feet long rose up some fifteen high and crashed down on the empty deck of the ferry.

The crowd cheered and slapped each other on the backs as they celebrated a successful launch. Andre beamed with the satisfaction of seeing his planning come to fruition.

Several men surrounded him and shook his hand.

Eric allowed himself a slight grin. He walked past the crowd and approached Bass. He stuck out his hand. "Excellent show there … Sorry, but I missed your name. Recall you hail from Sherman."

"Yassah. That be right." He stuck out a sweaty hand. "Bass Reeves from Sherman, Texas. I 'members meetin' you … back in Shreveport."

"Mighty brave of you two to step in and do what you did. What is you friend's name?" He glanced over at Bass's logging partner who was surrounded by well-wishers.

"Oh that be Chuck … Chuck Norris. He taught me a thing or two about usin' this here ax."

"You learned well. Understand we are having a fish fry tonight. With hushpuppies." Eric grinned as Bass' eyes got big.

"Oh I surely and purely hope so. Do not mean to sound ungrateful but some of these army meals ain't hardly fit fo' man o' beast." Bass shook his head.

"No arguments there. Have eaten better, and I have eaten worse," Eric said with a wry grin. Now if you will excuse me, I have some things to take care of."

§§§

CHAPTER TWENTY-SIX

EAST BANK OF THE MISSISSIPPI

Silver flashes of incandescent tentacles of lightning illuminated the inky blue skies from both north and south as the five skiffs approached the burnt out remains of Wilkinson Plantation, Mississippi. Eric held a coal oil lantern high over his head, shielding his eyes with the brim of his cavalry hat.

"Twenty degrees right gentlemen. I think I can see the dock Colonel Hebert was talking about."

Forty yards later, the first skiff bumped up against the weather beaten structure. Eric tied off the rope attached to the bow, picked up the lantern once more, and stepped up to the dock.

The second skiff bumped into the dock. Eric reached out and gave Colonel Hebert a hand. "Looks as if our luck is holding out."

"Indeed it is. First time in Mississippi?"

The young officer chuckled. "As a matter of fact ... Never dreamed I would have rowed myself here."

The four burly cavalrymen seated cross legged in the in the back of the first skiff to land began to get up and disembark. The first one out was carrying his rifle. He tuned to a another and said, "Johnny, hand me my saddlebags and soogan, would you."

The friend complied, making it much easier for the remaining men to move in the crowded wooden boat. Soon, all twenty of the rope pulling detail were off loaded and gathered around the two officers.

"Men, find a nice place to stretch out and catch a nap if you can. Lord willing, we will be back in about an hour with the rope, and your little holiday will officially be over."

His comments brought a few chuckles from the troops.

"We will leave three lanterns lined up on the dock. Y'all will have another three to move around in the dark over here. We do not know of any enemy troops nearby, but Sergeant Jackson is in charge. He may well decide to post a guard. Any questions ?"

One of the troops with a coal black beard spoke up. "Sir, I kinda feel naked without my horse. What do we do if the ferry idea does not pan out?"

Eric looked him straight in the eyes. In the weak light of the lantern glow, only the whites showed. "My orders were to get you across this mighty river and reinforce what is left of the Army of Mississippi."

He let his words sink in for a moment. "That being said, I will not abandon you here on foot with no supplies. That would not, in my judgment be combat effective. It would also be a waste of what I consider very, very precious ... your lives and well being."

He turned around slowly to look into the faces of all the men surrounding him. "We still have these five little boats at our disposal." He pointed back toward the dock. "If Colonel Hebert and I do not have the ferry operational by zero five thirty, I will return here to take you back to Arkansas."

"Thank you Colonel. We appreciate it more than you know," the bearded man said.

Eric shook his hand. "Wish us luck." He turned to face Andre. "Do we need anything to mate up the ferry to the dock as far as the wagons are concerned?"

"That is a good question. Perhaps a few wide planks to accommodate the drop from the barge to the dock. The river is rather high now. We shall see how low the ferry rides in the water when it is loaded."

"I will leave that up to you. My job now will be to get the rope and cable across the river."

Andre nodded. "Speaking of that, I wanted to point out the most eligible spot to anchor on this side. See that stationary gin pole? It is probably fifteen feet in the ground. I have seen it lift a sling with a half dozen bales at one time. The rope and pulleys are gone, but that big vertical shaft is solid."

"Good to know. We best get back across. Still have much to do."

Bass Reeves was admittedly nervous as the lantern lit road cut through the trees ended in almost pitch blackness. A light warm rain was falling, and the sky offered no clue as to the direction he was facing. He leaned to the right and saw a few men standing near what turned out to be the water's edge.

Past them, he could see a pair of lanterns about one hundred yards away. *Looks like they be movin'* Sure enough as he watched, he was able to make out the near end of the ferry he had helped launch.

Across the expanse of the black water, on the Mississippi River bank he could not see was a single spot of light.

Captain Reeves called out in a strong voice, "All right men, it is our turn. Keep your horses on a short lead and keep them calm."

The ferry docked, and two men detached a single heavy rope across the near side.

"Take it slow and easy now," the man commanded as he led the last of the Second Company down the plank road descending the cut made into the shear ten foot tall river bank.

Bass saw a familiar silhouette observing the loading process. As he walked past the slightly taller officer, he called out, "Hey, Colonel Eric. That fried catfish tasted jest like home. 'Preciate them hushpuppies, too."

Schmidt turned to see the familiar smile on the muscular slave's face. He grinned as the que of cavalrymen continued to slowly pass. "Glad you liked it. They saved some for me as well … It was rather good, I must say."

"You comin' with us to Mississippi, Colonel?"

"Not yet. Maybe we will meet up again some day."

"Take care of yourself, Colonel. Bless you."

"And you too, Bass. God speed and protect you."

"Yassah." Bass moved on down the plank ramp holding on firmly to his mount's lead rope. "Easy does it, Whiskey. Ain't nuthin' to be skeered of."

He moved in tight with the other men and their mounts and could hear the moving water splashing against the left side of the ferry.

The other men and their horses blocked almost all the feeble light from the lanterns mounted on all four corners. Bass could feel his pulse begin quicken. The fact that he could not swim did not help a bit.

Bass stroked the horse's neck and began whispering in his ear. "It is fine, Whiskey. Jest a few more minutes ... we gonna be on dry land agin."

He looked over his shoulder as the last of the load for the ferry's fourth trip were marshaled aboard. Two men closed the rope gate and grabbed hold of the side fences for safety.

With a slight hiss of steam, the piston started the flywheel spinning again, and the operator shifted the capstan power transmission lever into gear.

Bass felt a slight lurch as the barge began to move. He patted Whiskey's neck in earnest. "Not too bad now, is it?" It was not readily apparent if he was trying to convince the animal or himself. "Say, did you hear that young colonel prayin' for me?"

Many miles to the east, he could make out numerous flashes of lightning in the far distance. Another huge bolt—spreading out like a silver spider across the dark super cell—demonstrated the awesome force of nature.

In his deep, low voice he began singing one of his favorite spirituals, "Swing low, sweet chariot ... coming fo' to carry me home ... "

Thirty hours later, the last ferry returned empty from Greenville. Twenty men from the Second Cavalry regiment eagerly awaited its arrival.

Colonel Andre Hebert supervised the crew responsible for disconnecting the barge and stowing it in the slightly curved channel connecting the oxbow to the muddy river.

"I want two lines on the upriver side. Secure them to the trees. Three full wraps around the circumference or the current will win that tug of war, I guarantee it."

Eric watched on the men take control of the craft and gradually move it laterally into the relatively narrow cut. He yawned as the first vermilion streaks of sunlight began to break on the eastern horizon.

Over a matter of minutes, the colors evolved

through shades of orange, peach, and pink as the stars faded and surrendered to the sun's light of day.

A flight of seagulls swooped along thirty yards off shore, skimming low and squawking—looking for an easy meal. One dipped its beak in the molten chocolate river and came up with a minnow.

Andre approached him. "You know, you really do not need to be here. When is the last time you got any sleep?"

Eric shook his head and tried to remember. "Um, I cannot say … exactly."

"Just as I thought. Your men have it under control. We will camouflage the ferry as we have discussed." He gestured back to where the dirt roadway morphed into an inclined ramp. "All those boards will be pulled up and stowed in the woods. No one will suspect a thing from the middle of the channel."

"You are right, as usual." He fought back another yawn. "I can take a hint … Wake me as soon as everyone has eaten. Really want to break camp as soon as possible."

"I know. The Yankees in Pine Bluff will not be fooled forever. Our departure from Tulip did not go unnoticed." He pointed down the road cut through the dense forest. "Go on, get out of here ... sir."

Eric chuckled. He stuck out his hand. "Thank you, my friend. We did it ... Could not have done this without you."

Andre beamed as he shook Eric's hand. "We make a great team, you and I. Now, seriously ... get out of here. I have work to do."

§§§

CHAPTER TWENTY-SEVEN

**TRANS-MISSISSIPPI DEPARTMENT
CONFEDERATE ARMY HEADQUARTERS
SHREVEPORT, LOUISIANA
APRIL 5TH, 1864**

"Colonel Schmidt, reporting as ordered, sir."

Major General Matson returned his salute sharply and with a huge smile. "I cannot tell you how happy I am to see you." He got to his feet and extended his hand. "It's been a busy month." He motioned to a padded chair. "Have a seat. I can fill you in on the latest." The look on Matson's face spoke volumes.

Eric sat his hat down on a nearby map table and slipped into the chair. "Ah, much better than that blasted bench seat on the train."

"As you can see from the hubbub out on the streets, Shreveport is not the same place you left last August. We are now the capitol of Louisiana, and have a huge target on our backs. Aside from that, I am no longer top dog here ... General Kirby Smith brought in a new two star to assume overall command."

"I saw General Taylor's name on a plaque outside the building. I assume that some greater priority arose over taking back the ports along the Texas Gulf coast."

"Just matter of priorities, and that is all. You and the men of the Second Regiment did a stellar job in Port O'Conner and Corpus Christi. If the Confederacy had a Navy, I would put you up for admiral."

Eric laughed. "Let no good deed go unpunished." He took in a deep breath and let it out slowly. "So, how may I help you?"

"General Richard Taylor has been placed in charge of all Confederate Forces in Louisiana at this time ... He just arrived here two days ago. Union General Nathaniel Banks is heading this way, moving up the Red River with his Yankee Army of the Gulf."

"Can we stop him at Natchitoches?"

Marcus shook his head. "Afraid not ... It fell into Yankee hands a few days ago on April 1st. A thousand pardons ... Sorry, I failed to mention that a fleet of Yankee gunboats is steaming up the Red supporting Bank's amphibious movements. Another division or more of Union cavalry, commanded by a Brigadier Albert Lee, are mixed with infantry, and artillery are working their way up the road that essentially parallels the river."

Eric's eyes narrowed. He gritted his teeth and processed the information. "We still have time to get more reinforcements from Arkadelphia and Tulip ... "

Mason shook his head. " Not so, I am truly sorry to say. The Arkansas cavalry at Tulip ran off without hardly firing a shot back in October of last year ... Abandoned all their gear."

"Son of a ... " Eric was incredulous. "I do not understand. Why would they simply cut and run?"

Matson shook his head. "They obviously did not have the stomach to fight. They later retreated southwest from Arkadelphia, and, at the present time, are in a small town called Washington. The Yankees basically control all the major towns down to and including Arkadelphia.

"We had an Arkansas cavalry regiment come down under Major General Sterling Price, but he took them back home when General Kirby Smith would not send them south to intercept Banks.

"There are still some brave souls up there, but in good conscience, I cannot place my trust in most of them."

Eric nodded. "I understand completely ... If Shreveport falls, the end is all but certain. What do you need me to do now?"

"We can step next door and I will introduce you to General Taylor. He knows of your reputation and will strongly consider your advice."

Both officers got to their feet. General Matson stopped before they got to the closed office door.

"One other thing before we go ... I am certain you will want to ride out and give the LeBlancs fair warning. If we do not stop Banks before he reaches here, their property and life's work will essentially be forfeit."

The image of a love-struck Angelina gazing up into his eyes flashed before him as Marcus' words cut like a dagger to his heart. "How much time do we have?"

Matson locked eyes with his protégé. "Three days ... Four on the outside. Time is of the essence."

"Our work certainly lies ahead. Let us go meet with this General Taylor. I have a couple of ideas that might work."

CHATEAU LEBLANC

Augustin and Angelina listened closely as Eric explained the situation pertaining to the approaching Union army.

"As we have seen or have had reported, the Yankees respect no boundaries when it comes to taking private property from captured territories. Really wish I had better news to share with you, but the grim fact is, almost anything that is not nailed down can be expected to be carted off as spoils of war."

She was obviously frightened and glanced to her father and then back to Eric. Augustin had a serious look on his face.

"You will not let that happen to us, will you?"

"Sweetheart, you know I will do anything in my power to protect you and your home. It is just that..." His voice trailed off, and he was forced to turn away.

"You have got to do something!" she pleaded.

"I am doing something, my love ... Came here with a whole army of Texas volunteers to fight the Yankees coming up the Red River Valley. We have a chance ... a very good chance ... to stop them, but I would be remiss if I did not warn you both of what might happen if we fail."

"How many days did you say we have?"

"Three, maybe four ... I will be leaving in the morning to attempt to slow down General Banks as best I can. There will be a decisive engagement, I can promise you that ... Of course I cannot tell you the exact nature of our battle plans ... To do so would put all of us at risk. As long as you know nothing, you cannot be forced to divulge information should spies or outriders show up here before the main battle takes place."

Eric could tell the news was hard on his young angel. She did not cry, but her tears were not far from falling. She held on to her father's hand tightly.

"I do not want you to go, Eric ... We need you here to protect us."

He took in a deep breath—His blue eyes seemed to pick up the color of his gray tunic. "Angelina, honey ... If I thought I could do any good all by myself, I would ... you know I would. But there are thousands and thousands of troops marching up here as we speak. They also have gun boats, and if we cannot stop them, they will be steaming right up into your back yard by week's end ... do you understand what I am saying?"

She nodded as a single tear rolled from her left eye.

"I shall see if we can get our most treasured possessions packed up and ready to be shipped into town," Augustin said somberly. "All of our cotton crop from last season is already sold and delivered. Just traded for some breeding stock, and we still have a considerable number of horses to consider."

"Understand, sir. I only wanted you to have the opportunity to be prepared. You may not actually have to transport your valuables unless the battle goes badly against us. The proximity of the Union forces will make time very critical if that unfortunate event occurs."

"How long can you stay?"

"Begged General Lane to allow me a twenty-four hour furlough ... Thankfully, he agreed."

Angelina wiped the tear from her cheek and sniffed. "In that case, I will do my best to be of cheerful demeanor during our time together. You always say life is too short not to savor the moment."

That night after dinner was finished, Augustin, Angelica, and Eric retired to the drawing room sipping on their preferred aperitifs. Candlelight provided the only illumination as the sun had long since set. Augustin settled back on a burgundy leather wing back chair.

Eric escorted her to a gold silk brocade settee, took a seat beside her, and tenderly held on to her hand. They all talked of the upcoming planting season for a few minutes.

"Sweetheart, would you mind terribly if I could spend some time alone with you father? There is something we need to discuss."

Her eyes darted from his to her father and back. She had no inkling of what that discussion might be, but smiled sweetly, and began to rise. He stood up first and helped her to her feet, giving her hand slight a squeeze as she turned toward the door.

When the drawing room door clicked shut behind her, Augustin sat his cigar down in the cut crystal ashtray atop the freestanding mahogany table. A wispy column of pungent gray smoke snaked upward and wound its way through the brass candelabra on the pie crust table top. He looked straight into Eric as he asked, "What is on your mind, son?"

"Sir, in the two years since we first met, I have come to have strong feelings for your daughter."

"Is that a fact?" Augustin's face displayed no emotion whatsoever.

"Yes, sir, it is. And I think it is safe to say that she has developed a fondness for me as well."

"Really? I had not been aware of that," he lied. "What are you intentions in regards to her feelings? As her father, I am obviously deeply concerned … her well being is utmost in my considerations."

"Understand, Mister LeBlanc. As you know, I do not come from a wealthy family … my means are modest, to say the least. Both my parents died when I was young and I have not even seen our little ranch in years. Not even sure it is still there …"

"Go on …"

"Sir, the crux of the matter is that I love your daughter very much, and I am seeking your permission to ask Angelina for her hand in marriage … I promise to love her and cherish her and do my absolute best by her … forever."

The older man settled back in the overstuffed leather chair—his face gave away nothing as he contemplated the request. He sat quietly for a moment, then leaned forward as Eric became more and more nervous with each passing second.

Resting his elbows on the arms of the chair, Augustin brought his hands together as if to pray, and then placed his fingertips against his lower lip.

Seconds passed as the two men studied each other carefully. Eric was certain he saw tears start to rim Augustin's hazel eyes.

Finally, he spoke, "Son, for the last twenty years, that young daughter of mine was all I had left to love after her dear mother passed on … I knew this day would come and I was …"

He stopped and took a deep breath before continuing. "For many years, I was afraid I would lose her as well … But, knowing how happy you make her gives me greater joy than you can ever imagine."

A wave of relief passed over Eric.

Augustin smiled. "I cannot think of another man so deserving of her love and devotion. You are brave, intelligent, considerate, and trustworthy … She and I both sensed that the first time we met. It feels now that I am not losing a daughter … rather, I am gaining a son."

Eric sprang to his feet, his face radiating his joy. He extended his hand. "Thank you, sir …Thank you. Promise you will not regret it."

"Please call me Augustin … or Father." He took the colonel's hand and shook it firmly.

They walked side by side to the French doors leading to the formal dining room. When Eric pulled them open, Angelina was standing right outside, smiling from ear to ear.

"Were you eavesdropping, my dear?" Eric asked.

She threw her arms around him and hugged him with all her might. "Yes … Of course I was! Did you think for one minute that I was going to let you get away from here without me?"

"Suppose not," he said as Augustin chuckled.

She released her bear hug and stepped back slightly. Angelina had a smile somewhat reminiscent of Mona Lisa's as she arched one eyebrow, as if to say "I'm waiting."

It took him a second to comprehend the meaning of the look. "Oh, right … Almost forgot…" Eric dropped to his knee and reached for her right hand.

"Angelina Michelle LeBlanc ... My beloved ... I love you with all my heart and soul. I promise to forever cherish and protect you, as long I shall live. Will you grant me the greatest honor on earth and marry me?"

Her green eyes sparkled in the candlelight as a huge smile came to her face. "Eric Schmidt, nothing would make give me more joy than to be your wife."

He rose to his feet and kissed her passionately as Augustin beamed his approval.

ARKANSAS RIVER FERRY CROSSING

Colonel George Reeves, commander of the remains of the Eleventh Cavalry—reduced by well over a third in eight months of heavy fighting—glassed the ferry as the sun set on a partly cloudy sky. "Looks like a dozen men providing security." He handed the telescope to Lieutenant Colonel Shaeffer, his executive officer.

Art shaded the lens with his kepi, less the sunlight reflecting off it give their position away. He elbows dug into the verdant green spring grass on the ridge some 400 yards from the river. "Yes indeed. They are lollygagggin' in the nice weather. I see a couple boys down on the riverbank fishin'. Have a single picket line for their ponies."

He scanned the area topography. "It is pretty open down there. Not much cover for an approach."

"I saw that", said Reeves. "Think our best bet is a night stalk on foot. There are only twelve of 'em."

"Just like Chickamuagua?"

"Without the hills and trees. Those poor departed devils must have been city boys. Never knew we in the woods with 'em." The colonel chuckled.

"Nonetheless, we gotta get across that river, and a handful of bluebellies are all that's stoppin' us. See no problem goin' in with blades … backed up with sixguns." He collapsed the telescope, and handed it back to George.

When dawn came, the rebels stripped the Yankee bodies of their gear and personal belongings. Sacks of flour, cornmeal, and coffee from the mess tent went into the nearly empty wagons, along with uniforms, firearms, sabers, and pouches of loose ammunition.

"Colonel, what do want to do with the bodies?" a skinny bearded corporal asked.

"Bury 'em in the river. Absolutely do not need buzzards circlin' overhead. People can spot them for miles. I sure would love to see us in Tulip by nightfall."

George called over to a more muscular man, "Master Sergeant Norris, you still have those khaki tan pants you picked up in Tennessee?"

"Yessir. In my saddle bags." Chuck pointed over his shoulder at his horse gazing nearby.

"Make absolutely sure you get all that blood washed off your hands." George looked him over closely. "Your neck, too. Must have caught a jugular vein when you took out that sentry ... In any event, I want you to ride ahead, and check out the situation in Tulip. Seems as if things are quite fluid these days, and I do not want to ride into a Union stronghold unawares. Is that clear?"

"Yes, sir. Will get out of this uniform immediately."

"One other thing ... Take Bass with you. He will make good cover. Leave your rifle in the cook wagon, as well."

"Yes, sir. If that is the way you want it, I will do it."

Bass held on to the reins as Chuck glassed the town of Tulip from a cluster of trees several hundred yards from town. He looked back over his shoulder to insure no one rode up behind them from Pine Bluff. "See anything important? Don't look like that camp is still there to me, but it be way too far away for me to be real sure."

Master Sergeant Norris got to his feet and stowed the field glasses in his saddlebags. "Do not see the Stars and Bars flying anywhere. The Confederate camp is definitely gone. No tents whatsoever. Think I saw a couple of blue uniforms walking out of the mercantile store. I am certain they had yellow stripes on their legs."

Bass' face was troubled. "What we gonna do?"

"We gonna get our butts back to the column quicktime. There one of our regiments posted here when we left last July. Ain't got a clue what happened, but beat up as we are, I cannot see the colonel riding in to ask."

He grabbed the reins from Bass and they mounted up. With a nod of his head back to the east, he and Bass worked their way onto the road, and spurred their horses into a rapid trot.

It was just past noon when Colonel Reeves spotted two riders coming toward the column. Both silhouettes were from big men. As they rode nearer, he could see that one was a black man.

He never halted the convoy as Chuck and Bass reined up and spun around to match the slower pace of the wagons. "Well Master Sergeant, what is the verdict?" George asked.

The blond haired former lumberjack shook his head. "Not good news, I am sorry to report. The Confederate regiment is nowhere to be seen. Did not see a single flag with stars and bars."

"Any enemy troop movements?"

"Yes, sir, as a matter of fact, I did. Spotted a couple of 'em meanderin' out of the mercantile ... Pretty as you please. They did not act like there were any rebels within a hundred miles, if you know what I mean."

Colonel Reeves nodded. "Not welcome news. Thanks for making good time." He turned to his right. "Art, you got any ideas? Pine Bluff is east from the intersection ahead. We know the Yankees controlled it. And besides, it is in the wrong direction if we want to get back to Texas. If Tulip is under Union control, that puts us in a fight, and we are running a little shy on powder and shot."

Art spat out his chew of well worn tobacco and wiped his lower lip with his riding glove. "I looked at the map of Arkansas while we were waiting to cross on the ferry. Reckon it is only a hundred and fifty miles as the crow flies from here to Texarkana. Too bad we cannot just go south, 'cause there ain't no roads in that direction."

Bass listened intently. He was nervous but found enough courage to speak, "Massa George."

"Not now, Bass. Can you not see we are in an important conversation?"

"But, Massa George …"

The colonel turned and glared at him. "Did you not hear me?"

"Not meanin' to call Colonel Art a liar or nuthin' but they be some roads runnin' south." He pointed that direction. "Maybe they not be on a map, but I jest seen 'em with my own eyes."

"What are you talking about?" George Reeves demanded.

"Wellsuh, 'bout four miles back a'fore we turned off on this here road, they be a big ol' cotton plantation on the south side. They got roads on either side of them huge fields, and they go plum out of sight."

Chuck spoke up. "He is right … I remember that place. Do not have a clue where they end up, but I could not even see the main house from the road. Imagine a local could tell us how to get to another road runnin' south."

Art mulled over the news. "He has a point. These farmers know this country better than we."

§§§

CHAPTER TWENTY-EIGHT

HEMPSTEAD COUNTY, ARKANSAS
APRIL 15, 1864

A bedraggled sandy-haired scout reined up as soon as he realized the game trail he had been following was crossing a well traveled road. He backed his bay mare into a thicket and tied off her lead rope to a wild plum tree.

Slowly, he eased his way down to the road and studied it for tracks. Countless hoof prints and wagon tracks had been made in each direction. He took out his compass and checked true north. *This here road must be the one from Camden to Hope.* He was trying to estimate the distance to Hope when sounds of horses approaching broke the mid-morning stillness.

He slipped back into a large cedar bush a few yards from the edge of the dirt road and pulled the aromatic branches closed behind him.

Three riders approached—riding line abreast and joking with each other—until they were close enough for him to see their faces.

Each was carrying a rifle strapped across their back and wore a uniform.

A smile came to the bearded face of the scout. As they passed by, he eased out of his hiding spot, stuck two fingers in his mouth and whistled loudly.

They turned and looked back over their shoulders as he hollered out, "Wait, up, boys!"

The closest cavalryman whipped out his Colt and pointed it at the man who had startled them. "Show yourself! Who goes there?"

The scout already had both hands in their air, showing that he had no ill intentions. "Master Sergeant Chuck Norris, Eleventh Cavalry, Texas Volunteers."

All three riders closed the distance to Chuck. The senior man, a sergeant eyed him suspiciously. "You lost ... or some kind of deserter?" Venom dipped of every word.

Chuck bristled. "No, I ain't lost, you ignorant ass ... I am a scout, and I would appreciate it you showed a little respect to a superior enlisted man. This road runs from Camden to Hope, to the best of my map reading skills."

The sergeant nodded. "Well, at least you ain't completely lost." He thumbed toward the northwest. "Hope is twenty miles, more or less, thataway. Who are you scoutin' for?"

"As I said, Eleventh Cavalry."

"We heard you, but there ain't been no Texans up here in purt' near a year ... Lot of Yankees, though, and you might jest be one of them spies."

Chuck shook his head. "Yankee spies whistle you boys down a lot these days when you ride by?"

The corporal riding in the threesome spoke up. "Hey, Sarge, why would a Yankee spy call us over for a talk? That do not make any sense at all."

He turned to his left and scowled. "Shut yore face, Willy. If'n I want an opinion from you, I will ax for it." He mulled over the situation for a moment.

"All right, mister so-called master sergeant ... where is yore outfit and where are y'all a comin' from?"

Norris was beginning to get more than a little annoyed at the man's tone of voice. "My boys are 'bout a mile back ... maybe less. There is some thick brush just this side of the Little Missouri."

"How did y'all git across it? They ain't no bridges thataway." The sergeant was insistent.

"There is now, leastwise since yesterday. We had build three different ones since we crossed the Arkansas River."

"The Arkansas? How the hell did you get that far north?"

Chuck grinned. "North? Hah! We crossed the Big Muddy almost up in Tennessee." His affable smile faded as he continued. "We fought at Chattanooga, Knoxville, and Chickamauga. Lost most of the men in the 12th Mounted Infantry in that slaughterhouse."

"Heard 'bout that one … We had over 16,000 men wounded or kilt there. What was yore take on it?"

"Stupid generals doin' stupid things … Ever hear of a Spencer Carbine or Colt revolving rifle? They stacked southern bodies three to five deep …" Chuck's voice trailed off—his eyes misted over slightly, and looked past the three Confederates in a somewhat distant thousand-yard stare.

The sergeant glanced over at his compatriots. They both nodded—their eyes beginning to tear up as well. He swung out of the saddle, and took off his riding glove. "Sorry, Master Sergeant … Norris is it?"

Chuck removed his glove and shook the man's hand firmly. "We are headed back to Texas to resupply and recruit some replacements … gettin' mighty low on food and ammunition."

"How many are there in your regiment?"

"As close as I can tell, just under three hundred left out of six hundred."

"Y'all best follow us back to meet General Marmaduke. We have been bird-dogging a whole

Yankee division under a General Steele. Ran his ragged butt out of Arkadephia ... but could not stop him from retreatin', and capturin' Camden today."

"My God. Sounds we just missed those two opposin' armies. We traveled almost due south from road between Tulip and Pine Bluff ... At Princeton, we got some information from a local about that General Steele marchin' his army down from Little Rock," said Chuck. He pointed back down the game trail.

"That is when we made the decision to stay off the main roads and how we ended up right here."

GENERAL MARMADUKE'S ENCAMPMENT.

Colonel Reeves called a halt when the procession was a quarter mile from the sprawling Confederate camp. "First Sergeant, have the guidon bearers display the colors, please. When we ride in, I want every single soul to know who we are. Have the men hold their heads up high for Texas and the fightin' Eleventh."

"Aye, sir. As you wish." He snapped a salute and rode back to the supply wagons. When he returned, he carried two flags furled and encased in canvas tubes. He handed them to the designated flag bearers, and they promptly unfurled the tattered and battle-scarred Stars and Bars along with a Texas flag.

Reeves bellowed out his commands in a strong clear voice, "Eleventh Regiment ... In columns of three ... Forward at a trot ... Ho!"

Brigadier General John S. Marmaduke, commander of the Cavalry Divisions in the Trans-Mississippi Department of Arkansas had received word from one of his scouts about the unexpected arrivals.

He stood outside his tent, his long brown hair and beard danced in the stiff spring breeze. A smile came to his lips as the columns rode past, and Colonel Reeves saluted him with his saber.

General Marmaduke came to attention and returned the gesture of respect.

When half the column had passed in review, Reeves called it to a halt and had his men dismount. He, himself, rode back and approached the command tent. He sheathed his saber, dismounted, and strode to face the thirty-one year old brigadier.

George slipped off his stained riding gloves and came to attention. "General Marmaduke, Colonel

George Roberston Reeves, Eleventh Texas Cavalry, at your disposal, sir." He snapped a crisp salute, one that made the hard charging horse soldier grin as he saluted him face to face.

"By Harry, we are honored to have you join us, Colonel. I shall have my executive officer show your men to their campsites." He extended his arm and shook Reeve's hand before he turned back toward his tent. "Please step inside, I want you to meet General Maxey and Colonel Tandy Walker."

Reeves listened intently as the flamboyant and relatively successful cavalry commander laid out the situation.

"From intelligence we obtained from prisoners and the Union wounded, General Steele lacked a suitable plan of logistical support for this entire operation. Those poor bastards slogged in the mud on quarter rations ... marching down from Little Rock to Arkadelphia. There was not much for them to confiscate from the locals when they got there."

Reeves smiled. "Can certainly testify to that. It is far too early for summer vegetables and crops ... deer, and wild hogs are scattered, and hunted hard by the locals. We have less than four days rations in our wagons."

George shook his head. "We contemplated abandoning them a time of two ... you know, with the mud, and creeks and rivers we had to cross ... but the thought of no cook pots, and having to subsistence hunt for every meal was not at all feasible."

Marmaduke agreed. "You made the right decision. General Steele is boxed in over at Camden at the moment, and I guarantee that there is no extra food there. The whole dang town will be starving in two days."

"What is your situation vis a vis provisions?" George asked.

"Plenty of beans, corn, and a fair supply of eggs. Not much meat unfortunately ... A couple hundred porkbellies, a few dozen hams, and maybe fifty corned beeves. Have plenty of hardtack, but that God awful stuff is the last resort ... No fit meal for a fighting man." Marmaduke made a face at the thought of the rock hard-biscuits.

"So, General, do you envision a siege of Camden?" Reeves inquired.

"Heavens, no. We will allow them to starve for as long as it takes to force them to make a move. Then, God willing, our combined forces will pounce like the hounds of hell."

Colonel Reeves mulled over the information. "Sir, do you have any idea of Steele's objective in his campaign?"

General Marmaduke sat back and grinned. "Happy you asked. Apparently, the Union put together a huge operation aimed at a final knockout blow in Louisiana. Shreveport was their target, and Steele's expedition was to come down from the north in a gigantic pincher move to meet up with Banks and Admiral Porter from the south." He used his hands to emphasize his words.

"Up the Red River, I presume?" Concern was etched across the colonel's face.

The brigadier continued, "We received a dispatch early this morning that the invasion was beaten back soundly just south of Shreveport by forces under the command of our General Taylor."

He pointed at Reeves. "Some of them were your fellow cavalrymen from Texas."

"Thank God for that. Shreveport is key to keeping us in the fight," replied George.

Colonel Tandy Walker had been relatively quiet since the briefing began. "I have two regiments of Choctaw braves who are dying for a chance at a little retribution with these bluebellies."

He stared directly at Colonel Reeves. "You may not have ever heard of the Treaty of Dancing Rabbit Creek from back in 1831 ... Most folks have not. Some of my senior men are actual survivors of the forced relocation and starvation. The rest are descendants of the survivors. The *Trail of Tears* is no footnote in some dusty history book for them."

"I understand. Hate can be a very powerful force. Sometimes, it can even overcome a man's fear of death." He glanced at Marmaduke, who simply nodded his agreement.

§§§

CHAPTER TWENTY-NINE

OUACHITA COUNTY, ARKANSAS
LEE PLANTATION
APRIL 18TH, 1864

Union Colonel James Monroe Williams, Commander of the 1st Kansas Colored Infantry, a regiment made up mostly of former slaves, was quite satisfied with the results of his armed foraging expedition. His thousand-man combined infantry and cavalry force had filled—at gunpoint—over two hundred wagons with basically whatever foods were available in the rural farming communities and plantations some twenty miles northwest of Camden.

Tens of tons of golden dried corn kernels, still attached to the cob, glistened in the morning sunlight. Other wagons carried burlap sacks of the same precious cargo, mechanically separated by labor-intensive hand crank.

Still others were stacked with sausage, pork bellies, and smoked hams, taken over the ardent objections of the vastly outmanned and outgunned farmers.

He was particularly pleased that the Confederate cavalry that had plagued his men from Arkadelphia eastward was nowhere in sight. Five miles later, one quarter of the way back to the garrison town of Camden, the procession passed through the Lee Plantation.

Vast fields of harvested corn stalks, left standing fallow from the previous year's record crops, stood silent vigil to the blatant theft of the region's life giving food supply.

NO TIME TO DIE

Colonel Williams rode alongside the two black companies of his primary operational command. In front of them, a single regiment of cavalry and two other regiments of infantry wearily trudged onward.

Without warning, a host of gray apparitions arose from the dry corn stalks. A volley of deadly rifle fire rang out, shattering the tranquillity of the sunny spring day. All along the wagon train, drivers and their swampers fell victim to the furious fusillade.

Colonel Williams ordered the men of the 1st Kansas to protect the wagons at all costs. The men unslung their rifles from their shoulders and ran back to position themselves between the long line of gunsmoke and the immobilized wagons.

As the first round of sulfurous smoke began to rise in the still air, the black soldiers could see hundreds of Confederates feverishly reloading their muzzleloading rifles. They aimed and fired as they ran into position.

While they themselves reloaded, the horde of attackers let out a series of high pitched rebel yells, and began to advance toward the wagon train.

Down the field, some men stood up with battle flags waving, and charged forward, rushing quickly toward the heavily laden freighters.

Colonel Williams immediately recognized the iconic red, white, and blue colors of the Lone Star State. He cursed to himself and wheeled his horse around to check and see if his cavalry regiment was en route.

Thankfully it was, but as he watched, the signals of a dozen Confederate bugles blared in the distance—both in front of and behind the stalled convoy. A thunderous staccato of rifle fire came from the nine hundred mounted rebels that appeared, as if from nowhere.

Williams spurred his horse and drew his saber, attempting to lead his cavalry in a counter attack. His hopes faded quickly as his fatigued and ill-fed white infantry broke ranks and sprinted toward a swamp in the face of the overwhelming Confederate cavalry charge.

He was dumfounded by the absolute ferocity and scope of the rebel ambush. Williams reined back and spun around to see waves of screaming rebel soldiers—some shirtless and wearing what looked like war paint on their faces and chests—fall onto his surrendering black troops. Some of his men dropped their weapons and ran pell mell for their lives.

Others who had chosen to surrender were being bayoneted as he looked on with horror. *Oh my God. That one has an tomahawk!* He could not believe his eyes, and the rebel decapitated one of his men, and held the severed head high as he screamed something in a language that the colonel could not understand.

Hundreds of infantrymen in gray swarmed over the immobilized wagon train, as another five hundred Confederate cavalry galloped past them, and headed for the Union troops running for the safety of the swamp.

Colonel Williams used the flat side of his saber as a quirt, urging his mount to take him out of the path of the two converging rebel cavalry charges.

Almost as quickly as the ambush began, it was over. Colonel George Reeves looked on from a distance as the Choctaw troops stripped and even scalped some of the dead black Yankee soldiers.

He turned away—the gruesome sight sickened him. His trusted Executive Officer, Art Shaeffer, approached him as the carnage wound down. "Who was it that said, *'Only the dead have seen the end to war'*."

Brigadier General Marmaduke had his buglers recall his cavalry pursuing the defeated and starving Yankees. The swamp had taken away the tactical advantages of his cavalry.

He ordered the half dozen empty wagons to be burnt, and took over possession of the 197 full ones. The caravan reversed course with new drivers and headed west back toward Hempstead County.

The eighteen hundred Confederate survivors of the ambush at Poison Springs, as the battle came to be known, ate very well that night. General Marmaduke personally presented Colonel George Reeves with a bottle of bonded Bourbon whiskey captured in the raid—a welcome gesture of appreciation for the contribution made by the men of the Eleventh Cavalry.

It was almost 11 PM when the incident happened. Colonel Reeves had invited Bass to partake in a game of poker. He had done so on other occasions when bad weather curtailed military activities or he had become bored from the long days of riding.

George filled his shot glass once more and downed another shot of the straight whiskey. "Suppose it is my turn to deal again."

The two used toothpicks for currency, as Bass had no money to gamble away. The big man listened to the slurred speech coming from his master and checked out the level of the bourbon in the glass bottle. *Huh ... Near half gone already. All that shootin' this mornin' sho must make a man powerful thirsty.*

Bass took another sip from his canteen and replaced the stopper. The coal oil lantern hung from their tent's center pole helped ward off the cool night air. Outside, the camp filled with almost 2,000 cavalrymen was quiet.

George's eyes were becoming bloodshot. He fumbled as he shuffled the deck, mumbled a curse under his breath as he scooped up the well-worn cards back together and then shuffled again. The game was called five card stud.

Both men anted up two toothpicks. George dealt each of them one card, face down, and then a seven of spades to Bass, and an eight of diamonds to himself.

"Your bet," the colonel said.

"Bet a dollar." Bass tossed a single wooden sliver into the kitty.

"Dealer bets two." George added his share. He dealt a two of hearts to Bass and a nine of diamonds to himself. "Possible straight ... the bet is to you."

Bass blinked his eyes. *I swear that last one was from the bottom of the deck.* He let it pass as possible eye fatigue on his part. "'Nuther dollar."

George grinned. "Dealer bets three." He added them to the kitty. He poured himself another straight shot and downed it.

Bass watched more closely as George dealt the fourth card. It was a six of clubs—from the bottom on the deck. The colonel's own card was an ace of clubs. "Lucky day ... Ace is high. Your bet."

Bass bristled. In his right hand was a single toothpick, nestled underneath his middle finger and atop his index and ring fingers. As a fist formed, the toothpick folded and cracked. He stared his master dead in the eyes.

"I likes my cards from the top of the deck, i'fn you please." His voice was a low rumble, like boulders tumbling off a steep cliff.

George was taken aback by Bass' response. "You calling me a cheat?" His bloodshot eyes narrowed.

Bass did not flinch or back up an inch. "What I don't understand, is why, on God's green earth, would a man in your position ... feel a need to cheat a man in mine."

The colonel exploded. "Why, you uppity assed ..." He threw a sharp right hook to Bass' jaw across the tiny folding table.

Bass shook off the blow and tossed the table out of his way as if it were made of paper. Cards and the whiskey bottle flew across the tent as he lunged forward and connected with a crushing right cross to the colonel's chin. The powerful hit toppled the inebriated officer, and his folding chair over beside his cot.

The twenty-five year old slave flung the chair out of his way and scrambled onto his thirty-eight year old master's belly. Again and again, he pounded the man with all his might—a devastating left followed by a fearsome right.

George was unconscious and offered no defense whatsoever. Blood streamed from both nostrils, his lower lip was split, and both eyes would be swollen and black by morning.

Bass panted heavily as pure adrenaline coursed through his veins. He pushed himself back to his feet and stood there, mouth agape, panting as he looked down at his defeated master.

The repressed rage of over two decades of suffering under the abomination of slavery had boiled over into fight that lasted only seven seconds.

My God ... You went and did it now. You just beat hell out of a colonel in the Confederate Army. They gonna hang yore stupid black ass in the mornin'... That is, if'n they do not jest shoot you first.

Bass started to panic. He looked around to see what he could take with him. Remembering that it was quite cool at night, he knelt down and quickly rolled up his sleeping pad and bedding. He glanced over at George. The man was out cold, but at least he was still breathing.

He spotted the colonel's gun belt and cartridge box hanging on the tent pole. Bass lifted it off the peg and slipped it around his waist. He fumbled with the belt clasp for a moment, but figured it out, and pulled it tight. Turning the wick down on the lantern, he watched the flame slowly smother itself.

Bass peeked out the tent flap into the night. In the distance, he could see the cook fires that ran twenty hours a day to keep the regiments fed. With his saddle bags over one shoulder and soogan on the other, he slipped out quietly, carrying the hot lantern.

In a few minutes, he had made his way to the picket line. He had been given a replacement horse, as Colonel Reeves had his favorite mount, Dollar, shot out from underneath him at Chattanooga. As planned, George had taken Whiskey as his new mount.

Bass never really connected with his new horse and found Whiskey standing hipshot in the light of the waxing quarter moon.

"Hello, my friend. You 'member me, doncha?" he whispered as he rubbed the horse's muzzle and let him smell his scent.

Bass found his saddle and quickly got it rigged and cinched. By that time, the lantern had cooled enough to stow in his saddle bags. He tied them on, looked over his shoulder once again, and hurriedly tied the soogan down.

"Keep quiet Whiskey. We cain't be wakin' folks up," he murmured softly.

He took tight hold of the lead rope and slowly eased toward the camp perimeter. With only another forty yards to go to the tree line, he breathed sigh of relief.

His respite was short lived. A dark silhouette emerged from the shadow of a pine tree trunk. "Halt! Who goes there?" the sentry demanded.

Bass froze for a moment. He thought of the Colt .44 revolver hanging on his right hip. He had cleaned it for George several times, but never had the opportunity to actually shoot it. His heart almost stopped.

"Who goes there?" the sentry called out in a slightly higher voice. He thumbed back the hammer on his Enfield rifle and brought it to his shoulder.

Bass heard the clicks of the rifle's sear as the hammer came to full cock. He could tell the sentry had the rifle pointed directly at him. He swallowed at the lump growing in his throat and spoke weakly, "Bass ... Bass Reeves."

"Bass? What the hell you doin' out here, this time o' night?" The sentry pointed the muzzle upwards, held on to the hammer—gently lowering it back to half cock.

The runaway slave squinted in the dim moonlight. The sentry walked closer. Something about his body size and long hair looked familiar. "Richard, is that you?"

The eighteen year old from Corsicana chuckled. "Shore is ... You got any idee how close you jest came to gettin' shot? What are you doin' out here?"

Bass stepped closer where he could speak softly. "Runnin' away ... I did somethin' stupid and they will hang me, fo' sho.'"

"What did you do? Kill somebody?"

"Dang near ... beat Colonel Reeves half to death."

"Oh, Jesus." Richard tried to think fast. "Where you gonna go?"

"Dunno. Someplace they will never find me." He shrugged. "Indian Territory, maybe."

Richard thought for a second. "Take me with you ... I do not want to die like Michael did."

Bass shook his head. "Powerful sorry 'bout our friend, but I jest cain't. They will shoot you for desertin' … or hang you for lettin' me go."

"Come on, Bass, please. I am asking as a friend."

"Richard … you gots little brothers, a big sister, and nephews. Me … I gots nothing to lose." Tears rolled his face. "Ain't never had me no friend like you."

The sentry's eyes filled with tears as well. Bass dropped Whiskey's lead rope and extended his hand. Richard took it.

Bass blinked back the tears welling up. "I be so sorry."

"For what?"

"For this … ." With a single massive left hook, he knocked the young soldier unconscious. He caught hold of the Enfield in midair and gently lowered Richard to the ground.

He unbuckled his friend's cartridge belt and laid it across Whiskey's withers.

He glanced at his friend. "Could not come up with nuthin' else, Richard …This way, theys gonna mind I manhandled you and made my getaway."

Bass took one last long look behind him at the slumbering camp. He grabbed the reins and swung up in the saddle, carrying the rifle in his left hand. He walked Whiskey into the treeline and vanished into the dark shadows.

§§§§

EPILOGUE

INDIAN TERRITORY
APRIL 22, 1864

Bass woke up with a stabbing pain in his belly. It had been over eighty hours since his last full meal. A handful of wild onions and carrots that he had managed to find did not do much to fill him up.

He had avoided human contact, less someone turn him in to the Confederates. He rolled over to check on Whiskey—the sorrel was hobbled a few yards away, grazing on the deep grass beside the slow moving creek in the pecan bottom.

He glanced at his saddle. It and the bag were covered in a fine yellow powder. Reeves looked up into the trees. The leaves were fully formed and just behind them, the pecan branches were draped in skinny caterpillar-like pollen pods called catkins.

He brushed off his arms and got to his feet. Grabbing the sides of his overalls, he shook them and got off as much pecan pollen as could. He looked across the creek. *Wish it was a bit later in the year. Too dang early for berries and plums. 'Sides, I ain't seen nuthin' bigger'n a squirrel to shoot.*

Moving mostly at night and sleeping by day may have been safer but definitely was slower and less productive food wise.

Bass knelt down, and retrieved his canteen. He drained it, and then ambled to the water's edge to refill it. As he did so, he saw a shadow darting on the other side. *Dang if'n they ain't some fish in here. Ain't gots no pole, but I wager I kin make me a spear.*

He smacked the stopper tight on his canteen and began looking for a suitable shaft. There were no canes growing along that section of the creek, but he soon spotted a crepe myrtle on the far side, where the terrain rose up from the bottom land. He took the pistol and cartridge box off his gun belt, leaving only the sheath knife attached.

The hungry man ripped off his boots, wrapped the belt around his midsection, and fastened the buckle. Almost as an afterthought, he removed his tattered woolen socks and headed for the creek.

That ain't mor'n two feet deep ... leastwise, I hope that is all. He dipped a foot in. *Lawdy, that is some kinda cold. Must be spring fed.* Bass gritted his teeth and stepped in—sticky brown mud eased up between his toes. His breath came in short, shallow pants as he continued across the fifty foot wide creek.

Keeping his focus of the far bank, he pressed on, unaware of the hole in his path. It was not more than forty-five inches deep, but when the escaped slave stepped into it, the icy water went up over his belly. "Lawdamercy!"

Bass found it hard to catch his breath as the water reached his privates. He even used his hands to help paddle him forward on through the deepest part, and then ran as best he could to reach the far bank.

"Whoo…Did not think that was gonna happen." He stood on the dry land, shaking one leg, and then the other in a vain attempt to get shed of the cold.

It took longer than he had hoped to get the inch thick crepe myrtle shoot cut off with his knife. *Wish I had me that ax me and Chuck used back in Arkansas.* The thought of him missing his other white friend pained him somewhat, but he quickly forced the image of his buddy from his mind and focused on his task at hand.

He trimmed the small end of the shaft to a sharp point. *Them fish ain't all that big. It is not like I be stickin' me a wild boar.*

Taking the spear in his hand, he eased back to the water's edge. The sun was high at almost 11:00 AM, and he was not casting much of a shadow. He spotted a fish cruising parallel to the bank in eighteen inches of water. Bass crouched low as it approached and readied for the right moment to strike

The thrust was lightning fast but passed harmlessly over the fish—it sped away untouched. Over the next thirty minutes, the scene was repeated four more times. Bass was clearly frustrated by his lack of success. He sat down and pondered his problem.

He stuck the spear slowly towards a freshwater clam shell—apparently discarded by some raccoon that had dined on the delicacy many months before. As he watched closely, he noticed that spear appeared to bend as it entered the water. The point impacted the mud bottom was a good two inches above the clam.

"Dang If'n that do not beat all," he muttered in frustration. By accident, he had discovered what all indigenous people throughout history found out eventually—light waves bend in different mediums. He aimed lower and found the spear touched the shell.

Buoyed by his finding, he set back to fishing once more. On his second try, he speared a two pounder that shared his name.

Bass was excited by the catch—at least until he remembered that all his matches were in his saddle bags on the far side of the creek.

The return crossing was less eventful than the first. He cleared a spot and made a small fire. A few green limbs served as a spit, and he roasted the gutted fish—head, skin, and all.

Bass had a small sack of salt in the saddlebags, but no other spices of any kind. Once the fish was cooked sufficiently, he peeled the charred skin off with his knife and sprinkled it with salt. Holding the green skewer in his hand, he gnawed off a bit of the grilled bass. He savored the first bite, being careful to miss the tiny slivers of the fish's ribs, and backbone. "Thank you, Lord," he said before the took a second bite.

"You are very hungry," said a voice from behind him.

Bass snapped his head around. A thirty year old man was standing less than ten feet away, cradling a double barreled shotgun in his hands. He had short dark hair—his face was obviously used to working in the sun. In fact, he was dressed much like Bass.

Reeves glanced at his gunbelt and the Enfield propped against a tree. Both were out of easy reach. "Uh ... did not hear you walk up," he said.

"You were not supposed to," the man replied. "Smelled smoke from your fire ... came to see."

Bass was very nervous. The stranger did not appear threatening, but Bass was unsure of the situation. "You live near here?"

"Downwind." He nodded up the creek.

"Makes sense...Uh ... Would you like some fish? Can get me some more." He held it up to the man.

"No, thanks. My wife will make my meal. May I ask where you are headed? ... We never see strangers here."

Bass set the fish down and turned around to face him. "Do not rightly know. Are we in Arkansas?"

The man shook his head. "No, this is the Indian Territory. We are part of the Cherokee Nation."

Bass was clearly relieved. "Thank God ... I made it."

"What did you make?" the man asked.

Bass grinned. "Made it out of Arkansas." He slowly and deliberately got to his feet—his overalls still soaked from the creek. He looked directly into the Cherokee's eyes. He pointed his thumb at himself. "Me ... I was a slave to a Confederate Colonel. Beat him real bad 'bout four days ago, and headed west."

The Indian smiled, clearly impressed. "So, you are a warrior … You fought soldier chief for your freedom."

Bass slowly nodded. "'Spect you could say that."

The man smiled. "My Christian name is Ruben James. You probably could not pronounce my name in our native Cherokee." He chuckled to himself. He moved the shotgun, muzzle down, into his left hand, and offered his right to the bedraggled former slave.

The big man reached out and took his hand. "My name is Bass Reeves. So happy to meet you."

"It is honor to shake hands with a brave man," Ruben said. "Will you join us for dinner?"

Bass looked up before he answered. "Thank you, Lord Jesus, for listenin' to me." A huge smile came to his face. "Yassah, be right proud to join you and your wife."

§§§§

BASS REEVES,

LAWMAN

THE EARLY YEARS

by

BUCK STIENKE

CHAPTER ONE

CHEROKEE NATION
INDIAN TERRITORIES
APRIL 22, 1864

Bass tightened the cinch on his sorrel gelding. "Come on, Whiskey. We gonna walk up the hill a ways and visit with our new friends."

Ruben James, a thirty-one year old Cherokee, stood by patiently as Bass rolled up his soogan and tied it to the back of the Texas Hope saddle. A light northeastern breeze tousled his short, black, poker-straight hair as he smiled at Bass.

"Wager that creek was a bit nippy, this time of year," Ruben said as he looked at Bass in his water-soaked overalls.

"Testify to that … Man do what he have to do when he hongry … Good Lord give me that fish, but he sho' made me work for it." Bass chuckled.

Ruben was amused by the comment. "Ever since the temptation of Eve, we have to work to feed ourselves. Sometimes, we make what appears to be our own little Garden of Eden … but never is it the same."

His comment caused Bass to ponder. "Do y'all own this land we be standin' on?"

The Cherokee shook his head. "No one really owns the land. Land is eternal … Was here before we came … Will still be here long after we are both dead and turned to dust."

Bass considered what Ruben had said. "So, if nobody owns it, where do you build your teepee?"

Ruben burst out laughing. "Native tribes on the plains are nomadic ,,, Live in teepees. We Cherokee are what the whites call one of the *five civilized tribes.* My people have a written language. Dress like a civilized people and live in houses. Come, you see."

The farmer turned and tilted his head upstream.

Bass picked up the Enfield rifle and slung it over his left shoulder. Holding onto the sling with his left hand, he took hold of Whiskey's lead rope. He followed the shorter, but solidly built Indian up a path that followed the creek.

Topping a shallow ridge, the two men entered a ten acre clearing surrounded by a split rail fence. A Guernsey cow, four mixed-breed black and white calves, two horses, and a matched pair of mules grazed in the pasture.

On the far side, perhaps eighty yards from the creek, stood a single story shiplap wood house with a rock chimney.

Bass could see a barn and a couple of out buildings as well. "Build this all by yourself?"

"Oh, no ... Had help with the framing. Brother lives nearby."

"The fence, too? A lot of work went into that, I mind."

"No, did build that by myself ... over two seasons. Must have fences for milk cows."

"Mighty nice place you got, Ruben. How long y'all lived here?"

The man's face suddenly clouded. "Since I was six years old. Walked here from Georgia. My mother died ... little sister and two younger brothers, too. I remember was it was very cold and we were so hungry."

"Powerful sorry to hear 'bout your mama an' them. Must have been real bad." Bass' eyes rimmed with tears as well.

"Tribe gave us this section of land, and we started over." He shook his head. "But my father, he never was the same after *Nunna daul Tsuny* ... *The Trail Where They Cried*."

For the next one hundred yards or so, the pair walked in silence ...

§§§

BLACKSTAR ENIGMA by T.C. Miller

HISTORICAL FICTION WESTERN
THE NATIONS by Ken Farmer and Buck Stienke
HAUNTED FALLS by Ken Farmer and Buck Stienke
HELL HOLE by Ken Farmer
ACROSS the RED by Ken Farmer and Buck Stienke
BASS and the LADY by Ken Farmer and Buck Stienke
DEVIL'S CANYON by Buck Stienke
LADY LAW by Ken Farmer
BLUE WATER WOMAN by Ken Farmer
FLYNN by Ken Farmer
AURALI RED by Ken Farmer
COLDIRON by Ken Farmer
STEELDUST by Ken Farmer
BONE by Ken Farmer
BONE'S LAW by Ken Farmer
BONE & LORAINE by Ken Farmer
BONE'S GOLD by Ken Farmer
BONE'S ENIGMA by Ken Farmer
SILKE JUSTICE by Ken Farmer
NO TIME TO DIE by Buck Stienke

SY/FY
LEGEND of AURORA by Ken Farmer & Buck Stienke
AURORA: INVASION (Book #6 in the BEF) by Ken Farmer & Buck Stienke
BONE'S PARADOX by Buck Stienke

HISTORICAL FICTION ROMANCE
THE TEMPLAR TRILOGY
MYSTERIOUS TEMPLAR by Adriana Girolami
THE CRIMSON AMULET by Adriana Girolami
TEMPLAR'S REDEMPTION by Adriana Girolami

Coming Soon

HISTORICAL FICTION WESTERN
SILKE'S QUEST by Ken Farmer
McGRATH by T.C. Miller
BASS REEVES LAWMAN - The Early Years by Buck Stienke

HISTORICAL FICTION ROMANCE
DAUGHTER of HADES by Adriana Girolami
ZAMINDAR and the LADY by Adriana Girolami

SY/FY
ANTAREAN DILEMMA by T.C. Miller

Thanks for reading *NO TIME TO DIE*. If you enjoyed it, I would really appreciate a review on Amazon. My Author Page is:
www.amazon.com/Buck-Stienke/e/B0057XZNKW
Email - buckstienke@yahoo.com

Personally autographed books available at my web site: www.TimberCreekPress.net

TIMBER CREEK PRESS